TEGAN STONE

AND THE
GIBSON COUNTY
BEAST

Mark D. Trollinger

also by Mark Trollinger

Texans Investigating Mysterious Entities Series:

The Chupacabra and the Bat Rastard

Champ and a Bit of Sunshine

The Red Ghost and a Chocolate Bunny

The Loveland Frog and the Narrow Path

Tegan Stone and the Gibson County Beast

Other Books:

Corrè

Published by Myths and Malts Productions Chandler, AZ

The book is a work of fiction. The author drew the characters, incidents, and dialogue from his imagination and did not construe them as real. Some events from the original cryptid sightings have been retold, modernized, and at times, fictionalized.

This book includes the use of trademarks for realism. Product names, logos, brands, and other trademarks featured or referred to within this manuscript are the property of their respective trademark holders.

These trademark holders are not affiliated with the author or any of the author's representatives. They do not sponsor or endorse the contents, materials, or processes discussed within this book.

Drink responsibly and do not drink and drive

If you or a loved one need help with an alcohol problem, please reach out to SAMHSA's National Helpline: 1-800-662-HELP (4357).

The author will donate 15% of the sales from this book to the Loveland Learning Garden in Loveland, OH. I will make donations quarterly. See the *Field Notes* section at the back of the book for more details.

"Simply put, a modern-day Valkyrie is a woman who is an everyday warrior. Whether it's battling demons in the past, in the mind, or life events and stress, she's a Shield-maiden through and through. Strong and vulnerable, she's been wounded, yet she lives and thrives. Imagine a Valkyrie who comes down from the heavens extending her hand to others who are struggling in battle. She chooses to slay her demons, her battles, and lifts her sword and shield to help others who need it."

Modern Day Valkyrie

For the many truly strong, fierce, independent women in my life. True modern-day Valkyries who are everyday warriors and shield-maidens: my wife Susana, my daughter Karmina, my mom Linda, my mother-in-law Lydia, my grandma Ginny, and my friends Sobie, Marsha, Ronda, Holly, Kristina, Maggie, and countless others.

Stay true, continue the fight, and keep kicking ass.

Table Of Contents

1 Angry River

The sun hung just above a brightly colored orange horizon. Its rays temporarily blinded the driver of a Winter Chill Pearlcoat 2013 Dodge Dart, which caused her to react with a quick slam of the visor into its downward position. She slowed the vehicle as she entered the on-ramp curve to merge onto Evansville's I-69.

The highway traffic was heavier than most days, with what seemed to be an endless sea of aggressive drivers who exceeded the posted speed limit. The flow escalated the routine task of merging with oncoming traffic to an unnecessarily difficult one for the older-model car. A small, visible break appeared within the next wave of cars, which gave the driver the desired opportunity to enter that they sought. She met the recognition with a smirk as the driver mashed the gas pedal and entered the acceleration lane to match the speed of the freeway traffic. Despite the driver's pleas, the Dart failed to live up to its model's moniker and struggled to achieve the velocity needed to blend with the flow of traffic by the end of the ramp.

As the driver attempted to enter the freeway, a large red 2021 GMC Sierra hit the brakes and swerved around the Dodge invader. The truck's driver signaled his displeasure with the blare of his horn and an extension of his middle finger, both directed at the driver of the smaller car. He added an enraged mouthed vulgar comment and rolled down the passenger window to allow the driver to fully see the visual. The Dart's raised window muffled the truck driver's angry voice, and its driver continued without an acknowledgment of either activity.

The driver moved from the staging lane and took position in a through lane behind the angry truck driver, only to dart her eyes upward to the rear-view mirror to see another large, modified diesel truck approach rapidly from behind. Within seconds, only the grill and the top of the truck's headlights were visible in her mirror. She glanced in the driver's side mirror and recognized there was no room to escape into the other through lane. She released a sigh as she moved back into the slower far-right lane. The now angered driver of the second truck shot her an angry glance as he hammered down on the gas pedal to speed up and glare at the driver. As he forcibly accelerated, the truck rolled coal as it overtook the smaller car and left it enveloped in a dark plume of sooty, unburned fuel exhaust fumes.

Moments later, she reached the speed limit, but the driving conditions did not improve. The highway felt angry. Its cars passed in relentless waves that resembled the rage of a river as it chased down and tossed a helpless leaf stuck in its mighty

pull. Cars continued to drive aggressively and tailgate the smaller Dart, even as the driver proceeded above the posted limits.

"Sheesh! What's wrong with people today?" asked the driver aloud, despite riding alone. "Time to get that oil changed."

Tegan Stone dismissed the actions and emotions of the other drivers on the road and continued her journey to an early morning appointment at the opened Deaconess Clinic Behavioral Health on Fourth Street in downtown Evansville. She parked in a lot near the intersection of Walnut and Fifth Street, then fumbled through the glove box to retrieve a new disposable face mask from the pack inside. She affixed the mask over her nose and mouth by placing her left, then right ear through the mask's loops, and raised it above her nose. She looked at her watch to verify her early arrival for her appointment.

This wasn't her first visit to the hospital. That came a month ago, after her friend, Dr. Guy Kelley, referred her to Dr. Oliver Rowe after she informed him of her plan to move to Evansville. The past several weeks had been filled with darkness, confusion, and many unresolved questions. Dr. Kelley was a good friend and an excellent listener, but after spending six weeks living in a small casita behind his Cincinnati home, she decided it was time to venture back into the world and begin some intense introspection to answer her unresolved questions regarding recent changes in personal tastes and behavior.

After the initial consultation with Dr. Rowe, she returned two weeks later for their first official session together. It was an introductory meeting, but they discussed some issues she had that included bottled up feelings and suppressed memories. The therapist felt they could have better success unlocking mental barriers through hypnosis and memory recovery.

Dr. Oliver Rowe, or Dr. Ollie as his patients referred to him, was a psychiatrist with over twenty years' experience. His eyes were deep set and the color of blue tropical waters. His silky, straight, short hair was the color of coffee with cream and worn in a business-like style. Although his hair was short, his eyebrows were bushy and of similar color, with an added hint of gray. He wore a green-checkered button-up cotton shirt with tan, relaxed-fit trousers, but covered up the outfit with a white coat. When he was younger, he didn't wear the white coat, but over the years he found that most patients felt it created a sense of calm and safety between them and the doctor. It also helped facilitate a professional identity and served as a gateway to acceptance among medical staff and patients. His patients viewed the coat as a robe of compassion and a symbol of a caring nature they expected to receive from their therapist.

Tegan already felt comfortable with Dr. Ollie after her initial visit. Being in a similar profession, she knew what the job called for, and her expectations were high. His warm handshake and pleasant smile put her at ease, and his active listening without interruption solidified her opinion. The second meeting included discussing her career as a therapist and her participation in cryptozoology investigations. She described the excitement and nervousness she felt in San Antonio when the team investigated the chupacabra. Coming face-to-face with a creature she had thought only existed in folklore altered the paradigm of her worldview.

Although it was Ty who took the blunt of the creature's attack, she told the doctor how it charged at her, and her instinctive reaction spared her from injury. The trip to Burlington gave the team peace and an escape from the increased media attention and stress that came because of the summer investigation.

That peace was short-lived after reports surfaced of Champ and its sudden attacks on animals and small children. From there, the demands didn't stop. The team set up a new office in Austin and headed to Phoenix, where things really unraveled for her. She told Dr. Ollie that she thought she had understood the creatures they encountered, but just when she thought she had a grip, it spiraled in a new direction.

The supernatural entity that was the Red Ghost's rider commanded the undead camel to seek vengeance across the Phoenix area. That was unexpected, but the passageways beneath the dam in Dreamy Draw and the discovery of the abandoned alien spaceship and notes on countless cryptids and entities the government had investigated for decades were the key factors that triggered her anxiety. These were feelings she couldn't shake, even months after the incident. Those feelings stuck with her and affected her ability to investigate in Loveland. Instead of being able to investigate the area and focus on clues to solve a mystery, she was nervous and jumped at every unknown sound. She wanted to appear to the others that she was as comfortable as they were, at least Carson and Ty, even though inside she was not.

She could feel the anxiety and fear from the cryptid investigations carry over into her personal and professional life as well. She found it more difficult to help her clients to the degree she had prior to the start of this path into the unknown. She hoped Dr. Ollie could help her understand these feelings and return her to how she perceived life before San Antonio. The prior session ended with her discussion of Cincinnati and how the encounter caused her to step back from the team.

What happened in Cincinnati? she remembered Dr. Ollie had asked as time expired on their prior session. She described the rush of emotions she felt on the last day of the investigation and how she felt differently waking up the next day in the hospital. As she stood to leave, she recalled telling Dr. Ollie she felt as if there were more to her story, but she couldn't recall. Three days later, when he emailed confirmation for today's visit, he mentioned he wanted to try hypnosis. Tegan understood hypnosis was the subject of a great deal of research and debate. Many believe information recovered under hypnosis was judged to be less reliable than conscious memories. She also knew that information retrieved under hypnosis was not admissible in many courts of law. However, she also knew that she felt there was more than what she remembered, and she couldn't explain the changes she had felt since leaving Loveland.

Despite the uncertainty within the scientific community, she knew other studies showed hypnosis could be effective in helping individuals come to terms with traumatic or extraordinary experiences. Hypnosis may help people gain control over their pain and anxiety because under they found hypnosis, people gain insight through imagining and practicing new behaviors. If it could help her become more resolved in her day-to-day living and answer some questions she had, it was a procedure she was willing to explore.

Besides, her and her friends' adventures in cryptozoology were also considered to be fringe within the scientific community.

2 Hypnotic

The elevator dinged to signal its arrival on the third floor. Tegan exited the open door and turned left. Even though this was not her first meeting with the therapist, the location was still unfamiliar. She squinted as she ambled down the hall and scanned the wall's signage to locate suite 300. Once inside, Tegan headed to the front desk, wrote her name on the printed patient log, and took a seat in the waiting room. Ten minutes later, she was taken back to a patient room to await Dr. Oliver Rowe. After a quick double knock on the door, Dr. Ollie entered.

"Welcome back, Tegan. How are you today?"

"I'm good, Doctor."

He held direct eye contact through the greeting and extended his hand to grasp hers in a normal handshake. He slowed the handshake by pacing and leading Tegan's hand during the clasp, then shifted the touch and pressure until he slowly released the handshake.

In a slow, smooth, monotone relaxed voice he asked, "How's Indiana treating you so far?" while he maintained a gaze into Tegan's eyes, and left her hand buoyant.

"Still learning my way around, but so far, so good."

"Please, take a seat," he invited, maintaining the eye contact and monotone vocal delivery. "Relax. Breathing is an involuntary process, but we find by breathing in and out consciously, the stress melts away and allows you to feel more relaxed."

She took a seat on the room's sofa while Dr. Ollie sat in a chair to the right. She took in a deep breath, held it briefly, and then exhaled.

"You might like to close your eyes if you feel your eyelids getting heavier. Because you're breathing in and out deliberately, you can relax more deeply now," he suggested.

She continued to focus on her breath, and her eyes closed naturally.

"It feels good to relax. You've been very busy. I know you will do well today, because accessing the part of the mind where deep thought occurs will help reduce the stress you've been under these past few months. Learning is easy for you. You are not one of those people who cannot think, but one who is interested in how the mind works. In fact, I bet you could be your own hypnotist and enter a trance how it is best for you if you simply let yourself relax and enjoy this time," he said.

A hint of a smile crossed her face at the suggestion she was interested in how the mind worked and the acknowledgement that she was good at it. She was a behavioral and cognitive psychologist, and a good one at that.

"I am sure you feel a sense of satisfaction knowing you possess these skills, rather than sensing dissatisfaction or ambivalence. Now, focus on your hands. You may either focus on the left hand, that being the right choice, or on the right hand, leaving only one left. And notice how they feel," suggested Dr. Ollie.

Tegan's right hand moved, despite appearing to be in slumber..

"As one enters a trance, they often feel various sensations of warmth or even a tingling sensation as they relax. Though it is not uncommon to notice no change, and just can focus attention on the hands. As you relax, notice how you feel perfectly still. You can focus on those hands, either the right or the left, or even your feet."

Her foot twitched against the support of the sofa.

"Perhaps you notice the weight of the shoes on your feet. A sensation, I wonder, if you have paid attention to before? Your feet are elevated on the sofa and yet grounded by the sofa. Many people notice that this affects the feeling of the weight of their shoes, or even creates a sense of weightlessness. As you enter a trance, you may or may not notice several varied sensations. Or perhaps you will only experience the process. Anything is ok. This is your time. You are the operator. I am merely following your lead as you go deeper and deeper into a state of hypnosis," Dr. Ollie spoke comfortingly.

Tegan's body relaxed further on the couch and appeared to go limp. Her face reflected a look of satisfaction at becoming one with the couch. Dr. Ollie crossed his right leg over his left and studied notes of the prior session in Tegan's file. He clicked the record button on a small audio device and asked questions.

"You've had a lot of exciting trips and adventures over the past several months," he said.

"Yes," replied Tegan in a low, somnolent voice.

"What happened in Bozeman?"

"Don't know. Never been."

Dr. Ollie scribbled the response in his notebook before asking, "What happened in Santa Fe?"

"Never been there," replied Tegan, which caused the doctor to write additional notes.

"What happened in Oxnard?" asked Dr. Ollie.

"I was born there. Raised with my younger brother and sister by my mom," she responded.

"Just your mom? Where's dad?"

"Don't know. Gone. He moved when I was ten."

"That must have been difficult. How did your mom react?"

"It was hard on her. She struggled to appear to everyone that things were okay. She needed help. I helped with the kids."

"You were very helpful," replied Dr. Ollie.

"Yes. I had to."

"Why did you have to?"

"She was hurting. She needed help to keep up and get better."

"And you've helped like that your whole life."

"I try."

"And still today," added Dr. Ollie.

"Yes."

"As a therapist."

"Many clients."

"People who are hurting and struggling to make ends meet."

"They need help," responded Tegan.

"And your friends. Carson, Tyson, and Kareem."

"Yes."

"You help them too."

"I try. Sometimes I fail."

Jumping subjects, Dr. Ollie asked, "What did you want to do when you were a kid, but couldn't because you were helping mom?"

"To be a zookeeper," Tegan responded.

"Why?"

"I love animals."

"And what else?"

"Travel."

"You liked to travel when you were a kid?"

"Wanted to. We couldn't. I said one day I would."

"And now you have. We talked about the places you've been," continued Dr. Ollie.

"Yes."

Dr. Ollie continued to write in his notebook and dug a little deeper into Tegan's mind.

"What happened in Phoenix?"

The expression on Tegan's face went blank.

"Phoenix," she said with a slight wince on her face.

"You've been there, haven't you?"

"Yes."

"What did you see there?"

"Darkness."

"The darkness sounds peaceful. What do you see there in the

darkness?"

"A door. Underground below a dam."

"Is the door open?" asked Dr. Ollie.

"It's broken and ajar."

"Did you go through the door?"

"Yes."

"What did you find beyond the door?"

"A lab."

"What's in the lab?"

"Desks, samples, a filing cabinet…"

"What's inside the filing cabinet?"

"Files. Notes, research, articles. Investigations."

"Investigations of what?"

"Creatures. Mysterious creatures. And aliens."

"Aliens?"

"There's a… a notebook about aliens. And another door."

"What's behind that door?"

"A spaceship. In the lab. It's humming."

"Are you afraid?"

"Shocked. Standing and staring at the spaceship. Then I back out into the lab."

"You needn't be afraid. We are spiritual beings having a human experience and exploring our third dimensional world. These entities are higher dimensional beings exploring our third dimensional world," advised the doctor.

"Yes."

"They seek to observe and perhaps communicate, but also to learn. Not to harm."

"Sometimes."

"And you've been to other places as well, haven't you?"

"Yes."

"What happened in Loveland? What do you see?"

"Darkness."

"More darkness?"

"Yes."

"Is it the same?"

"No, it's different."

"What do you see in this darkness?"

"A light."

"What kind of light?"

"A blue light. Soft. Glowing."

"Can you see its source?"

"A being … maybe a man."

"A man? What's he doing?"

"He's floating."

"Floating? An emanating light?"

"Like an aura."

"They say a blue aura shows peace, a quiet order, and a person who speaks the truth."

"Yes."

"Someone who has a strong sense of purpose, is sensitive, and has a developed inner guide or teacher."

"He doesn't look like a man, but I feel like it is a man."

"What does he look like?"

"Like a Dementor."

"A Dementor?"

"Yes, a flowing black cloak, no face, no hands. Just a blue aura and he appears to float."

"What's he doing?"

"He's reaching out to me."

"Do you take his hand?" asked Dr. Ollie.

"Yes."

"What do you feel?"

"A pull."

"Then what?"

"I'm flying."

"Where are you flying to?"

"Darkness. Then a wooded park."

"Where is the park?"

"I don't know. I think Loveland."

"Who is in this park?"

"A man… a little man."

"Little man?"

"Just under three feet. Maybe smaller. Coming from the bushes. He's staring at me."

"Are you afraid?"

"No. I'm calm. He is staring and cocking his head."

"As if studying you or searching for an answer?"

"Maybe. He seems to find the answer."

"What does he do?"

"He touches my head."

"What happens?"

"A light."

"From the being in the blue light?"

"No, from the little man's hand. Purple light."

"Purple auras are often psychic and mystical with strong emotional connection."

"I can see his face through the glowing light."

"What does his face look like?"

"Like… a troll… bushy hair, big ears, big nose, small eyes. Red eyes."

"Can you feel the light?"

"It's… cold. Feel it enter my head. Tingling. And a bright flash."

"Then what?"

"I'm in the woods. I blink and I am in a hospital."

"Did the little man wake you and fly you through the darkness and into the hospital?"

"I don't know. I don't think so. The blue man flew with me to the park. The little man woke me. Dark again. I'm in the hospital."

"But you saw him in the woods?"

"Yes. The woods."

"What happened in the woods?"

"Running. I was scared. Chased. Then my body tingled like it was hit by something. Some kind of energy. Then I was grabbed by something. A large frog. It pulled me into its mouth. Then darkness."

"That darkness leads to the man in the blue light and to the darkness that ends in the woods with the little man in the woods again."

"Yes."

"What do you see in the space between the darkness and the blue light?"

"A light."

"The blue light?"

"Bright white light. And a being. Beings of light. Pure white light. I can hear them in my head. We have a shared understanding."

"Them?" clarified Dr. Ollie.

"Yes, there's more than one."

"Then what?"

"An obstacle. A blocked tunnel. Preventing me from going. Forced to turn around. Blue light."

"What do you feel?"

"A rapturous sense of serenity and bliss. All around. It envelops me."

"Then what?" asked the doctor.

"Then a thud. Like my body hitting a wall."

"What happens when you feel the thud?"

"I see my body lying on the ground."

"You see your body?"

"Yes. From the hill. Like watching a movie."

"What happens in this movie?"

"The guys are running around confused."

"Carson, Tyson, and Kareem?"

"Yes," answered Tegan.

"Why did you say earlier that you disappoint your friends?"

"I'm insecure and afraid. I feel like I don't belong. I'm not like the others."

"Imposter Syndrome."

"The chupacabra attacked me. I injured it and it attacked Ty. And the frogs. The frogs attacked me. And I died."

"You are not an imposter. *Ex opera operato*. It means *from the work performed*. In sacramental theology, it refers to the objective reality and effectiveness of the sacraments that are independent of the merits of the minister or the recipient. Here, you are performing the work of a cryptozoologist. You may not see yourself as one, but others do, and you are validating your journey through the work you perform."

"I was afraid."

"You were learning a new journey. It's okay to be afraid."

"I was weak."

"You survived. Ty survived. Everything turned out okay. And you are much stronger now. I know you are learning as you experience something new today. You will continue to learn more. You are stronger than you realize. You stood firm and faced your fears head on. You went to hell and back. Now you have defeated that fear and returned. You are a badass. Strong and independent. Death has changed you and you may find some things from your life no longer fit. Some people no longer fit. Maybe your job no longer fits. You have only seen the tip of the iceberg of your new self. Your journey is just beginning. Are you ready?"

"Yes."

"You are an incredible person who people love to be around. You make everyone's life better by being you. You are strong. You kick ass. You are fearless. You are ready to pursue the mysteries of life head on. Help others transcend their obstacles. You are a guide to others. You've always been helpful. Help them realize their true self and achieve higher vibrations. You are mystical and powerful. You are a fantastic hypnosis subject, and you can look forward to all the positive changes in your life," Dr. Ollie said.

"Yes."

"In a moment, I am going to count from one to five, and when I reach five, you will open your eyes. You will feel refreshed, relaxed, and fantastic. Ready to embrace your new life and the gifts it brings. Five. Four. Three. Two. One."

As Dr. Rowe reached the final number, Tegan opened her eyes, but remained horizontal on the sofa.

"How do you feel?" asked Dr. Ollie.

"I feel… incredible. Relaxed, but energized," replied Tegan. "How'd I do?"

"You did great. I knew you would. I learned a lot from our session today. I'll see you back here in a couple of weeks for another discussion.

Tegan stood and shook Dr. Ollie's hand. "Thanks, Doc. I'll see you then."

She opened the door and exited back into the lobby, feeling refreshed. She passed through the front door of the building and stepped into the fresh air. The sunlight warmed her face and gave her a feeling of rebirth and energy.

3 Necromancing The Stone

A sleepy hamlet with less than a thousand residents, Puyuhuapi, is one of the oldest villages in Chile's southern Aysen Region. With its forested shores of the icy Seno Ventisquero and natural hot springs, it's a peaceful village for tourists to soak lakeside in outdoor pools fed by the thermal waters surrounded by natural beauty.

Just twenty-four kilometers south of Queulat National Park, rivers wind through its fairy tale lush wilderness. Tourists often take the thirty-two-kilometer route to the famous hanging glacier, or *Ventisquero Colgante*, where they might see and hear the ice crash down on the rocks below. During the summer months, they could take it easy and hop on one of the small boats that navigate across the Laguna Témpanos to the glacier. Fifty-one kilometers south of Puyuhuapi is El Bosque Encantado, or Enchanted Forest. It is a moist, magical forest where people say gremlins and elves live. Tourists might encounter them if they take the hour's walk to where the glacial waterfalls drop into the river at Laguna El Duende.

Fifty-one kilometers south of Puyuhuapi is *El Bosque Encantado*, or Enchanted Forest; a moist, magical forest where visitors whisper rumors of living gremlins and elves. Tourists might encounter them if they take the hour's walk to where the glacial waterfalls drop into the river at Laguna El Duende.

While tourists sought to escape the toxic environment and problems of the outside world by visiting the Patagonian region, some locals seek an escape from their own life challenges, despite living in an area of immense natural beauty. Santiago Torres was one of those locals. Being twenty-four years old, he felt confined by the small fishing village. Puyuhuapi found a place on the world map and drew global attention as a new travel location. That created opportunities for tourism jobs, but those filled immediately.

He was fortunate to have a job as a busboy at a small restaurant, even if he didn't feel fortunate. At least it provided him with enough money to afford a small, one-bedroom apartment in an aging complex with poor lighting. The hallways were always dark when he returned home and lumbered down the hallway after a hard day's work. He didn't have a car, but the restaurant was less than a mile down the brick laid Carretera Austral. Some described it as South America's finest road, but to Santiago, his entire world was only a few square miles. He felt the walls surrounded him and limited him to this tiny bubble.

He dreamed that one day he would escape from this small town and see the world. Unfortunately, his wallet and his small dimly lit apartment told him it was not possible. The only time he felt a glimmer of enjoyment was when he sat on his dingy, burned orange sofa with a cold cerveza within arm's reach on his wobbly coffee table to watch Campeonato fútbol and his beloved Santiago Wanderers. At least the television, when it worked, provided a brief escape from his daily surroundings.

His world changed one night four months ago when a man stopped Santiago as he walked home from work. He still thought of that chance encounter from time to time. Late night, complete darkness shrouded the street. It was cold and windy as Santiago briskly walked toward his apartment. He walked close to the buildings, using them to break the sharp bite from the wind. It wasn't much, maybe not anything, but at least it protected him from the weather, and that's what he wanted more than anything that night. Still, he dreamed of an escape from his limited life in the inlet.

Lost in thought, he imagined he was somewhere else. Anywhere else. He looked up to see the apartment building was within in sight. Suddenly, a man emerged from an alley between a small row of shops. Cristobal stood near a trash can underneath a dimly lit streetlight that flickered more than it illuminated the darkness. Santiago didn't notice the man from the shadows as he approached and attempted to assess the bus boy's level of interest in his illicit sales pitch.

"Hey, man," Cristobal called out to him.

Santiago dismissed the man's message and continued to walk, hoping to ignore the interruption. The man kept pace and walked beside Santiago to continue the attempt.

"Surely you want to relax, homie. I see you working at that restaurant every night. Don't you want to unwind? Don't you want to get away?" asked

Cristobal.

The thought of those words stopped Santiago in his tracks.

"Get away?"

"Yeah, man. Get away. Escape this small ass town where nothing happens. There's nowhere to go. There's nothing to do," led Cristobal.

Santiago's thoughts again race to anywhere. Anywhere but there.

"Now that you mention it, yeah. I *am* tired of this place. I want to travel far from here," answered Santiago with an emphatic hopefulness.

"I know what you mean, my man. And I got just the thing you need."

"I don't know, man," he reconsidered as his mind raced. "Naw, I don't do drugs or none of that shit," rejected Santiago, as he shouldered past the hustler.

But the moment of hesitation showed Cristobal there was at least a microscopic level of interest, and that was a window of opportunity he could use.

"These ain't drugs, man. They're *synthetic*," he stressed in a calm, persuasive tone that made the stereotypical sales tactics of used car salesmen appear feeble. "It's a way for you to get out of here and experience the world. *You want to be here your whole life?*" the man questioned. "Think of what you're missing out there. You could go anywhere in the world. Hell, maybe even another world," quipped Cristobal with a short, half-suppressed laugh.

Santiago chuckled, "Another world. That's a good one. I'm good, fam'. Lemme get home before this wind gets worse."

"C'mon, just try it. What can it hurt? It's synthetic," the man persisted.

"Synesthetic weed?" questioned Santiago.

"No, this is better than weed. It's N-dimethyltryptamine," pitched Cristobal.

"I'm no scientist. What the hell is that?" "I'm no scientist. What the hell is that?"

"It's DMT, man. Some call it the *spirit molecule*. Weed gets you relaxed, but it doesn't take you anywhere."

"And this does? Take you somewhere?" clarified Santiago.

"Hell yeah. You'll leave this town in the dust."

"I don't know. I have little money," Santiago replied.

"It's all good, my guy. It's only ten-thousand pesos," Cristobal answered.

Santiago paused and thought about the transaction. That's when Cristobal knew he had him hooked.

"That's right. Just a small price, and I know you're pulling in money from working all those shifts," he encouraged. "You work so hard, don't you want to come home, put your feet on the table, and see the world? Don't you think you deserve that?" Cristobal encouraged. "I'll even throw in a free pipe."

The thought of escape stuck with Santiago. That was the one thing he desired more than anything. He scanned the street and didn't see anyone else around. Who would know? No one. And Cristobal was right about a couple of things: he worked hard, and he deserved to relax. The possibilities churned the gears of thought in his mind, and his position on the subject changed.

"You know what? You're right. Ten thousand is a small price, and what the hell? All I do is work," acknowledged Santiago.

"There you go. You deserve to put yourself first," encouraged Cristobal.

The realization that he worked hard, and he took very little time for himself, caused Santiago's body to display excitement as he thought about the possibility of leaving everything behind. He reached into his wallet and retrieved the ten thousand pesos. Before he completed the deal, he once again looked around to make sure no one saw the transaction. Confirming the coast was clear, he extended the money to Cristobal and simultaneously received a bag.

"Let me know how it works out," replied Cristobal as he retreated into the shadows after a fist bump.

Inside the comfort of his apartment, Santiago sat on the sofa and searched for the game on television. His mind thought about his experience after meeting Cristobal the first time. Santiago recalled he didn't try the product that evening, but waited a few nights later after yet another hard shift at work. His coworker, Saul, came over to watch the game with him and to serve as a trip sitter. Santiago knew Saul had experience using DMT, and to prepare for his first time, it felt more comfortable having an experienced traveler watch over him.

Saul packed the pipe for his friend and turned on some relaxing music in the background to set the vibe. He finished preparation of the environment to provide the best opportunity for a comfortable trip with the intention to explore the world outside of Puyuhuapi. Saul handed Santiago the pipe and instructed him on how to use it. He told Santiago to take three hits, no matter what, and received an acknowledgement and agreement in response.

Santiago lit the pipe and took a big hit. He was nervous, and it worsened as he felt a strong tingle, a numb-like wave, almost immediately rush through his whole body. It shocked him how quickly the reaction came. It startled him enough that he didn't take the second hit. He sat the pipe on a wet towel and sunk deep into the sofa. With just the one hit, he saw lights and colors. A lot of different colors, oranges, reds, and yellows. It made the world appear to be Play-Doh that melted and changed colors, like magma that exploded from the vent of a volcano.

As quickly as the hit affected his mind and body, it subsided, and he was back on the couch with Saul beside him. The entire journey lasted just over five minutes, but, to Santiago, it felt longer, and it provided a brief escape from his mundane life. He was still nervous about the drug, but also felt an eagerness to try it again. He invited Saul to come back the following weekend after he heeded his friend's advice to wait a few days between trips.

His thoughts drifted to the second night he tried DMT. It was a little easier because he knew how fast it came on, and a little more of what to expect. Or so he thought. The scene in the apartment was the same as the weekend before: the television played in the background, he played some soft music to set the mood, and Saul was there to watch over him. Again, Saul reminded Santiago to take three hits, no matter what. This time, Santiago felt confident he could do it now that he had one time under his belt.

He prepared the wet towel, lit the pipe, took one deep hit, and sat back on the sofa to await the sensation. He was ready this time and took in the euphoria for a moment before he took the second hit. But like his first experience, the intense reaction was greater than he expected. This time, there were more lights and colors. Instead of oranges, reds, and yellows, he experienced the surrounding landscape in bold blues and bright purples. He could only recognize it in his mind as something that resembled the shades of the desert sky at night. He noted everything around him was vibrant and alive. Everything moved and wiggled. It was an intense energy that felt alive and vibrated at a higher frequency.

He closed his eyes and basked in the new setting while attempting to soak it in. The shapes stood out as more than three-dimensional objects. They had multiple layers, like a floor that floated above another floor. He felt the shapes hover and vibrate around him in fractal patterns. During the initial period in this new world, he was not afraid, even though he discovered he couldn't move. He felt stuck and was unable to process the world around him. There was no panic, no sense of doom. But like the first trip, it faded, and he was back on the sofa. This time, when he returned, he felt an emotional rush. More of a genuine feeling of fright and confusion for five minutes after the trip ended. As he calmed himself, he acknowledged there were some lingering residual colors and feelings.

Back in the present, he took a sip of his Kross Golden beer and recalled the first time he broke through and could leave his physical body.

It was another weekend where Saul returned to be his trip sitter. Unlike the prior two attempts, this time he promised himself he would take three big hits from the pipe. He made it through the first hit, exhaled, then two the second. Waves of euphoria rushed through him, but he pushed through and took the third hit. And that's when it happened. The intense lights and colors returned, but this time, he felt a very heavy feeling in his body. Like his prior attempt, he could not move. Instead of accepting it, he struggled and fought with himself to move. He pulled and pulled and somehow detached himself from his heavier body. And he detached by flight. He flew high and fast, straight up to the ceiling. He looked down to see his physical body at rest on the couch and Saul beside him in front of the television. The screen flickered.

Sensations of exuberance rushed over his body. This time, the things he saw were shocking and sometimes scary. He discovered his conscious astral projection caused a much greater energy to flow into his astral self.

Trying to make sense of it, he looked around his surroundings. He felt as if his astral self was formless, like a floating figure. He couldn't see his appearance, but he caught a glimpse of a black flowing cloak, similar to the Grim Reaper. But he also sensed a strong energy. An energy that caused him to radiate a vibrant blue form.

He looked at his hands and noted the blue glow around their outline. Then he looked through his hands, further below, and again saw himself and Saul on the couch. Freedom overtook his mind, and he pushed himself to see where he could go. Milliseconds later, he sped meters above the earth's surface and over the ocean. He couldn't believe the freedom, speed, and excitement he felt. He guided his astral form away from the ocean and to the Eiffel Tower. As he flew in rapid circles around the Tower, he realized he could indeed escape his tiny village and travel, all much cheaper than a plane ticket. And more realistic based on his salary. The sensation of a dopamine tidal wave crashed down on his helpless soul and caused him to not resist the experience and thrill he felt.

Once again in the present, Santiago took another sip of beer as the memories returned to the background of his mind. That was the first trip he released his astral form, and it was wonderful. He recalled his pulse and heart rate increased; however, he never felt alarmed or scared. It was so enjoyable he tried it again. And again. And again. Each time, he focused on the euphoria of the trip and learned how to improve the experience. Along his journeys, he saw strange things: elves, aliens, and plants. Not just plants, but an alien jungle.

The drug's feelings and experiences hooked him and he decreased the gap between his projections from more than a week down to just a couple of days. The more he projected, the more he saw and the longer his trips lasted. He encountered light beings, interstellar beings, and beings from other dimensions. He learned how to communicate with these entities and to physically interact with them. He saw many humans on the astral plane who projected as he did. Some from the usage of psychological drugs, and some through meditation. Other humans traveled the astral plane while their bodies lay in a comatose state in earthly hospital beds. There were also others who had crossed over from their earthly experience and left their shell of a physical body behind.

He recalled the first time he discovered he could physically contact another while in the astral realm. It was a time when he flew aimlessly and basked in the freedom from the constraints of time and space. Suddenly, he crashed into someone and felt the physical effects.

I can feel others? he thought to himself.

You can if you focus, replied an unknown telepathic voice.

Shocked, he spun around to locate the voice's source, eventually noticing a tall, humanoid figure. It was bipedal, but he classified it as humanoid because he could tell it wasn't human. It looked like a caricatured version of a human with extended arms, legs, and fingers, similar to Jack in *The Nightmare Before Christmas.* The being's appearance startled him, but he was not frightened. The fact he could hear its thoughts inside his head frightened him more.

"You can talk to me?" Santiago replied aloud, before mustering up the strength to speak to the being telepathically. *Who are you?* he mentally projected.

You're getting there. More focus and your message will become clearer. You have a powerful energy about you, answered the being telepathically. *My name is Malakai. You're new here. I haven't seen you before.*

This is the first time I have been able to break out, projected Santiago. *I don't know if I am doing it right.*

It becomes easier with more experience. Soon you will do it on command, and through continued practice, you won't even need those human drugs to do it. There is more to see. I will guide you and teach you the ways of the astral realm, answered Malakai.

After another sip of beer, Santiago recalled working with Malakai on interactions with the other beings and human explorers in the astral realm. As he got more comfortable, he found the astral realm was about increased knowledge, understanding, and wisdom, not some horror movie, video game, religion-generated threats and promises. As with any collective of life-forms, some were benevolent, and some were dangerous. There were dark entities on the astral plane. If a traveler roamed enough, they would invariably come across positive and negative entities in the same way they would if they roamed the streets of any earthly city.

He discovered multiple dimensions, some with pure energy found in higher realms that often took the shape of light beings or angels. He found all light beings were attempting to help humanity because they felt we needed to grow. These higher dimensional beings contacted the human world and tried to show us the light. They wanted humans to ascend as a collective, but there were also darker beings that held a hell-bent anger to destroy humans. Shadow beings, elementals, and demonic beasts roamed the lower dimensions and sought to disrupt human life.

While the light and dark beings battled across dimensions, there were other creatures Santiago encountered on the astral plane. Mysterious creatures, often described on earth as cryptids, visitors from interstellar worlds, and beings from other dimensions. Then there were the elves, gnomes, trolls, and later the Pukwudgies.

Near the midway point of the bottle, Santiago recalled the first time he met Puddlesquat.

It was another night after a hard day at work. He arrived home to discover his cable wasn't working. He projected to pass the time. That night, while he explored, he discovered an astral world covered with thick astral forests. It was dense and dark from a lack of light. Perfect for good intentions and dangerous actions. Santiago saw an astral form that looked human, like him, and attempted to reach out, but there was no response. That puzzled him.

A being teleported next to him and told him it was useless to contact the entity. The visitor informed Santiago what he observed was deceased. When a human died, it was incapable of understanding its surroundings for several weeks. While departed humans were unaware of their new world, Santiago learned, through guidance from his mentor, Malakai, it was possible for him to reach them on the astral plane.

He placed the empty bottle on the coffee table and recalled the many experiences he had with other creatures. Not those who died and were temporarily in the astral realm, but creatures who came there with a purpose. To learn, to explore, and to engage. Creatures from other dimensions, like the Rocemur from Canter's Cave, aliens from other worlds across the galaxy, beings made only of light from before the earth existed, and physical beings that existed at higher frequencies, like the Pukwudgie.

The Pukwudgie, those mischievous creatures! Santiago felt it was fun to watch them torment humans and drive them crazy, but there was something about them that was endearing. Somehow, he knew that, at one time, Pukwudgies and humans were friends. Then humans broke that trust, and the Pukwudgie turned against them. There were always exceptions, of course, but commonly, Pukwudgies wanted to trick humans into injury, or worse. Along his journeys, Santiago learned they had an empathic side and were resourceful. Despite their mischievous reputation, he had a soft spot for them.

After observing many humans, he learned the ability to differentiate between purposeful astral explorers and those who were unaware they were in the astral realm. The latter were the deceased or comatose patients.

I wonder if I can touch them? he thought as he recalled the accidental experience of crashing into another astral being.

He recalled that the entity told him to focus his thoughts. Once he discovered he could physically touch them, he worked with Malakai to learn how to harness his energy in the astral world, focus it on an individual, and convince them to return to the physical earth with him.

He returned to the couch with a fresh beer, and nodded his head as he took a sip and reflected in the acknowledgement that the ability was exciting. He remembered asking himself how many people who wrongly died could he help? He recalled pondering those thoughts for days. Then days later, with another hit, he experimented.

His first attempt ended in failure as Santiago tested his theory and attempted to retrieve a human. Somewhere during the process, the two became separated, and he lost the person to another astral dimension. Santiago awoke on his couch feeling a large, sudden jolt within his body. He was unaware of the failure, but Malakai sensed it and warned the astral traveler not to become reckless with the lives of others.

He analyzed his experience and focused on his ability after it occurred to him he might profit from his skills. Loved ones would pay handsomely to have their loved ones returned from the dead. But if he were to make money, he must master the process. Malakai cautioned him again, but realized his young pupil was stubborn and would attempt it again. Malakai realized if Santiago was going to ignore his mentor's warnings and do it anyway, he might as well do it with proper guidance and training.

Santiago realized that his first attempt failed because he and his target became separated. He worked through the scenarios until he devised another plan. He returned to the astral plane and noticed another traveler who was there before her time. He flew down close to her, focused his energy before he reached out with his astral hand, and took hers in his grasp. There was a sudden flash of light, and he was back home on his couch. In his head he saw the image of the woman, in a hospital bed in another part of the world, open her eyes. Whatever event she experienced that caused her to leave her body was now undone by his use of the astral plane and proficient use of his abilities. The success motivated him to continue working to perfect the technique.

Soon, the process became easier for him, and his success rate became flawless. Again, he fantasized about people paying him to retrieve a loved one that left the world prematurely. That would help him leave his town for sure, and without the synthetic psychedelic drugs. He felt dirty meeting Cristobal in that alley any time he needed more, but what could he do? He couldn't purchase it in public, and he needed this. He was performing good deeds and helped families in despair.

As he continued to practice and perfect his ability to grab a human and return them to earth, other beings in the astral realm called him *Necromancer*. Often seen with a relaxed hooded jacket and jeans over his astral frame, Santiago became a rising star in the astral world. Astral beings saw him as one of the few who could physically interact with both the earthly and astral world.

Those who witnessed him grab an astral body, end his trip, and return to earth, reuniting both his and his passenger's astral forms with their physical bodies, marveled in shock at the speed at which Santiago learned the ancient skill of necromancy. He basked in the ability and increased notoriety that came with the successful return of a deceased human to their earthly body. Even if the human experienced a rather harsh impact on the return. Despite the success, he wished that there was a way to locate worthy souls more quickly. He realized faster trips meant the opportunity to help more individuals, and that meant more money.

That's where the Pukwudgie came in. Santiago learned that Puddlesquat, a Pukwudgie, possessed abilities that would help him locate dead or comatose humans quicker. His full name was Eilif Puddlesquat, but everyone called him by his last name. Santiago felt close to Puddlesquat and enjoyed his company. They formed a partnership to work together and help those who needed it the most.

Puddlesquat possessed the ability to see into the future, appear and disappear at will, the ability to turn invisible, to confuse people and make them forget things, shapeshift into animals, create fire, launch poison arrows, use magic, and lure people to their deaths, if need be.

Puddlesquat scouted situations where he sensed impending death, but rarely intervened. Instead, he would teleport back to Santiago to advise him of the events. Santiago didn't always project to save someone. Sometimes he did just to escape Puyuhuapi. He was a loner who enjoyed solitude, and having the ability to do what he wanted. Although he still hadn't learned to fully harness the power of the DMT, he loved the astral realm and the ability to experience unknown places and beings. He found Puddlesquat to be attuned to what belonged and did not belong in the astral realm.

Puddlesquat could identify travelers who were there intentionally, or those who did not belong. Those in the afterlife remained there until their time was called to return to the source. Most were unaware of his presence and still in a state of shock from their transition. Many didn't realize they were dead and resisted interaction with astral beings. This was especially true for those whose time had not yet come. The longer they were dead or in a coma, the more difficult it was to return them to their physical bodies.

The next time Santiago projected, he met Puddlesquat near an astral lake and where he learned of a new situation. There was an astral child who walked along the astral path. He could tell she was not one of the mysterious higher frequency creatures or someone visiting through meditation because she had not yet discovered the ability to fly. She was an unknown visitor. Santiago flew toward her and attempted to draw her attention. He greeted her, but she remained quiet, then returned a perturbed look on her face. Nevertheless, he knew what to do. She was a kid. She didn't belong there.

A kid should never be there. It must be a mistake, he thought.

He took her hand and flew through a tunnel, and then closed the astral door behind them. It was another successful mission. Both he and the child opened their eyes and learned they were back on earth. The recollection passed, and he drained a last sip of his second beer while sitting on his couch.

Growing up, he was always told drugs, and especially psychedelics, were bad. Since his recent experimentations, he learned how powerful of a wake-up experience it was, and he understood why the control system banned them. The system does not want people to fly off out of their body and into other dimensions and realities where they could see just how much support there was in these other dimensions. Puddlesquat was one of those helpful support beings he encountered. If it weren't for his encounter with Puddlesquat, he would not have learned to focus his ability to retrieve the dead from the astral plane.

Each time he projected, he was aware and present, able to see, hear, touch, smell, and taste the world around him. He discovered that after he began projecting, he experienced life with greater consciousness and vitality, knowing that he was more than just a physical being destined to lead a short, physical only, finite life in a small fishing village.

He retrieved a third Kross from the refrigerator and sat back down on the sofa. It was another dark and slow night in Puyuhuapi. A perfect night to kick back, relax, and surf the astral plane. Santiago turned the Wanderers' game on for background noise, then prepared to make another journey. He reached into the bag and noticed he was nearing the end of the remaining crystalline DMT powder. He would have to visit the dark alley again soon.

He packed the remaining crystals into the pipe Cristobal gave him with the first purchase, sat back on his sofa, struck the lighter, and held the flame to the pipe. He took in a deep inhale, then sunk deeper into the sofa. The effects of the synthetic DMT kicked in rapidly for Santiago. With his continued usage, it took less than four minutes to take the three hits and receive the initial wave.

He took the second hit, then the third. So peaceful, his astral body floated to anywhere he wanted on the entire globe. It was freedom. He knew they clinically tested DMT in depression treatment, but he felt its sensational release was also an area of opportunity for study.

Within five minutes, the wave of euphoria rushed over him, and he felt his body float and break out of its earthly shell. Depersonalization, the detachment within the self that allowed him to see things as an observer of his physical body, was one sensation he loved. Next, the hallucinations came. Or were they hallucinations? They seemed real, and he had experienced the return from the astral realm with a fellow traveler, therefore he knew they were real. As were the mysterious beings he encountered on the journey. Puddlesquat was certainly real.

The more he traveled, the more he encountered beings who were not human. They welcomed him, communicated with him, shared ideas with him, and he often returned home having had profound experiences. His experiences were esoteric experiences, and just as real as the physical world. He found connecting with a spiritual dimension and its beings transformed his mind as they showed him wisdom. The astral world didn't require his belief in it. It shattered his view of how reality worked, regardless of if he believed it or not.

Tonight's events began much like prior evenings. It was a dark and drizzly walk home after work and he just wanted to relax and escape. In his apartment, he set the mood and prepared for the journey. He no longer needed his friend Saul to watch over him. By now, he was a master and could handle any situation on his own. He packed with pipe from a fresh bag from Cristobal and prepared to settle in for the evening.

One quick hit, followed by a second, and a third. He no longer had to give a lengthy pause between hits. He knew what to expect and very few things surprised or derailed him from his intentions now. After the third hit, he projected to a peaceful place he liked to visit and relax. A place that had no drama, no unrealistic expectations, and nothing out of the ordinary, unlike the real world. He was ready for a relaxing night in the astral realm, unbothered by anyone or anything.

Then he saw a familiar figure, Puddlesquat. He informed Santiago of a situation in a faraway wooded area that caused a young woman to suffer an untimely fate. A fate that placed her in the astral realm long before her time.

At first, Santiago didn't want to save anyone today. He planned a quiet evening after another long shift at work. He just wanted to explore the realm and relax. He felt a universal intelligence fed him information and downloaded wisdom that he didn't know existed. He saw negative thoughts as dark green and black twisted patterns, but noticed when thoughts turned to positive thoughts, the patterns changed and blossomed into beautiful bushes. They were so beautiful and fragrant. They caused a warm feeling to encase his body. Tears began running down his cheeks. That's where he wanted to spend his time.

After he saw the beautiful images, he accepted that he should listen to Puddlesquat and save the girl. It was like he was the new messenger and helper of the universe, or multi-universes, and if he didn't play along, those universes grew angry and some of the darker entities would appear. He realized a bunch of other shit in other dimensions were around us all the time, but we don't have access. Through the DMT, he could access them. Death was one of those things, and through his experiences, it was no longer scary. He knew that there was more to life than our physical bodies and being confined to wherever we were living. It was much bigger than anyone could imagine. But if it wasn't our time to die, we didn't belong there, unless it was through a temporary journey such as DMT, meditation, or breath work could provide.

Fine, let's check out the girl, Santiago said telepathically to Puddlesquat.

Projection into the astral realm and the sudden return home were always an emotional journey for him. It affected him for hours after his return. Moments after finding the girl, he was back on his couch. He wept, he laughed, and smiled in his dark apartment with the Wanderers game on in the background.

"Damn, losing again," he said as he grabbed the bottle and took a sip of his beer.

4 Sweet Dreams Are Made Of This

Late at night, Tegan sat on the sofa of her Evansville apartment. She attempted to find something interesting on television and surfed through the channels. If nothing caught her attention, at least she had a snack to keep her occupied. She relaxed with a spoon and pint-sized package Ben & Jerry's Change is Brewing without a care. With the first taste of the cold brew coffee ice cream made with marshmallow swirls and fudge brownies, it transported her back to the Waterbury factory in Vermont, where she and the rest of the T.I.M.E. team explored the Flavor Graveyard during the vacation in Burlington. At least it was a vacation for a few days until Champ reared his head and drew them to Lake Champlain.

She continued to search the channels on her streaming device before she stopped on ESPN+. A soccer game was still early in the first period, and although she wasn't a soccer fan, something compelled her to stop and watch for a few minutes. She didn't recognize the teams or any players, but determined it was somewhere in South America. She hit the information button and read it was a match between two teams of the Chilean Football Federation, Everton de Viña del Mar, and one of the oldest soccer teams in the Americas, the Santiago Wanderers, founded in 1892. She watched it in Spanish. Not that she understood Spanish, but she didn't understand the game anyway and found the Spanish commentary team raised the level of excitement. She didn't look at the clock, but gauged time by the level of ice cream consumed. She always had an enormous appetite and would not stop until the pint was empty.

With an audible and continuous series of scrapes from the spoon against the paper bottom of the pint, she ensured she consumed every bite. It put an end not only to the pint, but to her night as well. She tossed the empty pint into the trashcan as she walked into the kitchen and then into the bedroom. She crawled into her bed, pulled the blankets up, burrowed a spot into her pillow, and prepared for a good night's sleep.

Although she nodded off on the sofa before she headed to bed, she found it difficult to fall asleep. She couldn't get comfortable, and instead suffered from frequent tosses and turns for the better part of an hour. She found a satisfactory placement within the large queen-sized bed and drifted off.

Almost immediately, she dreamed. It was dark, and she was outside. She sensed it was cold, and in her bed, she reacted with an unconscious reach and pull of the blanket up tighter over her shoulder. She felt warmer and snuggled down into the mattress as her mind explored the scenario.

She saw a thick forest on a hill, fallen foliage and aging, rotted bark on the large trees that surrounded her. She felt the cold intensify by a hard rain beginning to fall. Her body shifted in discomfort in the bed. The forest's canopy opened and allowed the moonlight once again to escape the dark clouds to peek through, causing the darkness to retreat. She saw herself with Ty, Kareem, and Carson as they explored the wooded area. But she was a watcher who viewed the scene as if she saw a movie. The team continued to push up the hill despite the conditions. She heard a rustle from behind and spun around to gaze toward the shrubbery. She thought she saw a shadow in the bushes. Something moved, but she couldn't make it out in her dream. She heard Kareem say he heard noises all around him, but he couldn't see the source.

She realized where she was when her attention turned toward two Xeephines off in the distance. She heard Kareem say he heard something unseen scamper through the leaves. In her dream, the point of view was that of a watcher, and through her dream eyes, she saw what was causing the noises she and Kareem heard on the hill that night. The source stayed out of sight from the team and remained under the cover of bushes, but now she saw what it was. A little man. Or was it a creature? That she couldn't tell.

She focused on the object in the bushes. It looked like a troll, or perhaps a leprechaun. She saw it was a humanoid creature about two to three feet tall, grey skinned, with large fingers and an enormous nose, and coarse black hair. While she attempted to study the creature in more detail, the point of view in her dream shifted back to the hill and the Xeephines. Not the two she saw from a distance, but another one came up from behind and chased her. One who attacked her with sharp teeth and a thick, saliva-covered tongue that knocked her forward as she attempted to run. She saw the guys turn around, but they were too far from the creature to help. She watched as she unbuttoned and slipped off her coat to escape, but the success only lasted for a minute.

She observed her body turn around to face the attacker as it stood staring at her; its long pink tongue retracted into its mouth, filled with jagged teeth. Its wide maw smacked and slurped in anticipation of eating its target. She watched as her physical body turned and ran, attempting to escape once again, but the creature gave chase and caught up. While her body was running, her dream observer saw the small creature under the bushes raise its hands and cast a wave of energy that struck her and caused a strong tingle sensation to rush over her. She could feel the energy throughout her body as she lay in slumber in the bed. Her physical body reacted with a shift in position.

The rush was short lived as she saw the tongue again smack into her back. Her body again shifted in bed as if it had just felt the force from the impact. In her dream, she cried out in fear as it yanked her backwards towards the visitor's open mouth. She saw herself claw at the ground to get a grip on something to free herself, but the soil was too soft, and the leaves were loose. The stickiness of the creature's tongue held fast on her back, and she could not slow the attack as the alien closed the distance between her and the creature.

She attempted to fight and scream, but it was no use as the creature pulled her into its mouth and closed its massive jaws. She saw the mouth engulf her. Its flesh covered her on all sides until she disappeared inside the creature.

She jerked in the bed and let out a whimper, although she remained asleep. She saw Kareem remove a weapon and fire it at the creature that ate her as Ty and Carson fought with the other two visitors. Her killer soon disintegrated from Kareem's weapon, and she saw her still body as it lay on the ground while the other two visitors teleported out of the grasp of the men.

The scene in her dream showed her the guys' reaction as they rushed to help her, and she saw the small troll-like creature disappear. She wondered about the troll and why it was there. It watched from a distance and appeared to use magic, but didn't physically intervene. It appeared as if it knew what was going to happen, but allowed the act to occur. She watched as her body lay motionless on the ground for several minutes.

She saw a blue light that blinded even her dream avatar. It glowed brightly, but she could not see from where it came. She no longer saw her friends around her body, and it didn't appear the scene took place in the woods. As her vision returned, she two piercing blue eyes without a face, but sensed a hooded man surrounded by a blue aura. She felt as if someone grabbed her hand, felt a dizzied flying sensation, and then a sudden jolt that caused her to sit up in her earthly bed. She felt confused by the dream as she looked around the dark room and tried to make sense of it all as the sweat dripped from her forehead and she felt a pain in her back.

5 A Change Is Gonna Come

Tegan awoke to a gray, wet morning as she stepped onto her second-floor apartment's small balcony. It was fitting, given her mood from the near sleepless night. She suffered from hypersomnia and couldn't shake the weird dream from her head. She often had difficulty remembering dreams once she awoke, but last night was different. It caused her not only to toss and turn most of the night, but the last portion of the dream jarred her awake and remained fresh in her head… and her back.

What happened last night? She remembered the Xeephines in her dreams, beings she never hoped to see again after her experience in Loveland. But what was the small creature and the glowing man in the hoodie? She didn't have an answer, and she couldn't recall them from prior dreams. She tried to take a mental inventory of her facilities, but the strong wind and sharp raindrops against her face prevented her mind from allowing her to drift too far from the three-dimensional world around her.

That she could still vividly see her dream from last night wasn't the only thing that felt odd this morning. Seemingly no longer bothered by the rain that now increased into a downpour, instead, she was overwhelmed by a sense of nodus tollens, a realization that the plot of her life made little sense to her anymore. At least, until recently, when she thought about life and her future, she felt she followed the arc of her intended story, but now she found herself immersed in passages that she didn't understand, and that didn't even seem to belong in the same genre.

She searched her mind and tried to uncover more of the disappearing dream. She recognized she would need to visit Dr. Rowe soon to discuss the nightly visions. The longer she was awake, the more rapidly the dreams withdrew into the darkness of her mind. She remembered the being in the blue light and the Xeephines. She knew they were real, although she found she suffered from rückkehrunruhe as the entire trip to Loveland was fading from her awareness. The memories felt more like a dream rather than an event that happened. Some images and feelings emerged from time to time, but they often felt out of place, as if they were pieces of someone else's puzzle. She ran her right hand through her thick, back-length red hair as she contemplated the visuals she saw in her mind. And she smiled.

"How's that?" the stylist asked as she turned Tegan's salon chair toward the mirror.

As she did earlier in the day, Tegan ran her hand through her hair, this time she examined the new style: bangs, a close-shaved undercut on both sides of her head, a long strip of her bright red hair cut in a Mohawk, and three long, thin braids, each woven through four Runic alphabet hair beads on each strand. The stylist pinned the long top portion of her hair up while she finished the hair tattoo design in the undercut on her nape. The stylist finished the geometric shape by razor, unpinned the hair, and allowed it to fall in the center in a thick, but narrow mane. She pulled it together in the back and clamped it with a Fenrir wolf head hair band that allowed the back undercut and hair tattoo to be seen. The silver fox contrasted with her bright red hair well.

"I love it! It's the first thing that's felt right in weeks," she said with enthusiasm.

As she left the salon, Tegan glimpsed her reflection in the door's glass and smiled. It was a fresh cut that boosted her mood and confidence. She wasn't sure why, but it made her feel fearless. She was ready for her next stop, just four doors down at a tattoo parlor called The Inkubus.

She opened the door and was greeted with a smile and cheerful salutations by Agnete, the young Norwegian tattoo artist Tegan spoke to four days ago when the idea of a tattoo first entered her mind.

"Good afternoon, Tegan. Love the hair," Agnete stated with enthusiasm. "Did you decide which of the two designs to get today?"

"Yes, I'll go with the smaller one today," Tegan answered.

"The one for the back of your neck?" clarified Agnete.

She turned to a desk beside her station and removed a manila folder from the drawer.

"These are the designs I sketched out. What do you think?"

Tegan reviewed the artwork, the first of a snake Ouroboros with the tree of life in the center. It reminded her of the investigation in Phoenix with the Red Ghost. The symbol represented the circle of life and death, and that was a connection to her experience in Loveland.

"I love the detail in that one. Your artwork drew me to this shop," she admitted.

"Thank you," replied Agnete. "Here's what I came up with for the tattoo for the back of your neck, and that hair style will showcase it well," she said as she handed Tegan a sketch of a tri colored Valknut, a Norse symbol of Odin, which translated to Knot of the Slain Warrior. "I drew each of the intersecting triangles in a different color: shades of orange, blue, and green. Fire lies inside one triangle, which highlights a brave, fiery character. Blue waters adorn the second triangle. And the third triangle comprises a lush forest."

"It's beautiful. The colors and symbolism speak to me for some reason," reviewed Tegan.

"Sweet. Let's get started," Agnete said as she led Tegan back to her station to prep her for the Valknut tattoo.

Tegan walked out of the tattoo parlor a few hours later and then headed to the nearby post office to retrieve the past three days' mail from her PO Box. She knew it was likely only bills and junk mail, but she received a phone notification that showed a small package was delivered earlier in the day. She knew she needed to retrieve it before the mailroom workers gave her grief about her habit of allowing the mail to pile up.

She arrived and unlocked the small box. As expected, her first order of business was to remove the suspected coupons, flyers, and bills from inside. She glanced at the front of each piece of mail. Nothing stood out as important and was deposited in the trash can next to the metal boxes. A gleam appeared in her eye and a smile appeared on her face as she noticed the small, brown cardboard package stuffed in the back of the box. Although she struggled to wiggle it from the small opening, she succeeded and smiled as she thought about the contents. She heard great things about Sucreabeille and was eager to try some new perfume, especially after her prior favorite scent attracted the primal aggression of the Xeephines.

Who knew a perfume could lead to one's death? she thought as she walked the box to a nearby workbench and prepared to open it.

Inside, she found three one-ounce bottles. She picked each one up and read the label, careful to double check the label to ensure there was no inclusion of benzoin. She remembered checking as she placed the order weeks ago, but she examined the bottle to verify there wasn't a mix up. The name of the one she wanted was Memento Mori. It reminded her of the small store in Ohio where the team visited on their last day together. It was there she reflected on her experience in Loveland and decided she needed to stay behind. However, maybe fittingly, it contained benzoin, which was what caught her in that predicament. Even though she wanted it, she didn't order it, but instead found others that sounded more fitting to her newly developing mood. And they were benzoin-free.

The first bottle, Bog Witch, included scents of a black, mossy, wet bog that dripped with fungi and subtle brushes of Artemisia, Atlas cedar, carrot seed, and labdanum. A hint of animalistic musk. The second bottle, Blood and Bone, contained scents of a dark forest at night. Moss and cypress, blood, and warm fur with a whisper of gun smoke and a drop of sweet resins. The last bottle, Something Wicked This Way Comes, combined bourbon, fresh tobacco, aged vanilla, a blend of patchouli and leather, earthy air, and a cafe mocha spiked with rum.

Satisfied with her shipment, she placed the bottles in her purse and headed to a last stop at her local favorite record store, Vinyl Forest. Since her move to Evansville, she had begun building a small vinyl library. It helped to connect her with the nostalgia of her youth. Lately, she found herself drawn to other genres outside of her standard Top 40 pop hits she had enjoyed since her teenage days. Now she noticed more hardcore music that created an aggressive, primal mood in her. Bands such as Arch Enemy, Abnormality, and Girl Scout Hand Grenade.

Although she did not find any new albums for her collection, she found herself drawn to a black tank top featuring a likeness of Maria Franz of the Danish, Norwegian, Germanic experimental folk band named Heilung. The group performed songs based on texts and runic inscriptions from Germanic peoples of the Bronze Age, Iron Age, and Viking Age.

Their instruments included items that were available to humans in the Iron Age, such as drums, bones, and spears. Tegan was drawn to Franz's image as an antler-wearing pagan mystic playing percussion with skeletons and bones. She was uncertain why she was so drawn to a band she hadn't heard. But her interest was piqued, and she saw a shirt in her size. She looked at it for a minute, snatched it from the shelf, and proceeded to the counter, where she also found a pair of cheap, dark sunglasses.

Back in the car, she changed into her new shirt, put on the sunglasses, and caught the reflection of her hair in the rear-view mirror. It was late evening, but not yet too dark to wear the sunglasses. Thinking of her shirt, she searched her music app and found the band's catalog.

Might as well check them out, she thought as she reviewed the song options from the list. Her finger hovered above the phone's surface before it stopped and played Krigsgaldr. She felt this required rolled down windows that allowed the wind to blow through her hair.

Driving home, the details of her dreams last night were long gone as she became lost in the earthy, medieval, tribal sounds of Heilung. It was a new style of music for her, but one that was mesmerizing and seemingly a call to action. But what action?

Back home later that evening, Tegan stretched out across the sofa and searched the channels once again. The glow from the television provided the only illumination in the room. The plastic Oreo tray crinkled audibly as she plunged her hand into the package to remove another handful of cookies. She liked to twist them apart, scrape the icing off with her teeth, and eat each cookie portion one at a time. It was the same tactic she used as a kid. She enjoyed them dunked in milk, but most of the time she didn't have a glass close at hand.

It wasn't long before a louder sound replaced the crinkle as her hand collapsed on the top of the bag, and she again succumbed to the late-night comfort of the sofa. As before, she found herself in a dream state and visions appeared. They didn't seem to form a cohesive story, but individual short clips in her head.

Again, glimpses of the Xeephines and the confrontation on the hill appeared. But this time, the focus was more on the little man in the bushes rather than the Xeephines themselves. When she was in Ohio, she didn't see the little man. Now she viewed the dream from a different angle. She soon realized that it was a lucid dream where her avatar could see her physical self again fall to the Xeephines in battle, but could move closer to see the little man. She felt as if she was watching a movie. She could see and interact with everything, but they could not see her.

Upon closer inspection, just mere feet away from the small man, she could tell it wasn't a man, but a creature. It resembled a human, but was much smaller. Only two or three feet tall. Its features were unproportionate with an enlarged nose, long fingers, ears, and hands. He had shoulders that sagged, a stooped appearance, and a tendency to hunch forward when he moved. Its hunched back was wildly hairy, covered in black coarse hair that resembled porcupine quills. Despite the creature's build, it still appeared to be agile. It wore a set of arrows in a quiver on its back, but she noticed while it possessed weapons, it was obvious the being had special powers. Her theory was confirmed as she once again observed the being release the purple light that seemed to glow from the palm of its hand.

She didn't know what the purple light was or why the small creature watched her. Dr. Ollie said purple represented healing. She watched the creature's hand glow and release a ball of light that traveled toward her. At that moment, just as it had happened yesterday, she felt the ball of energy strike her. Once again, her physical body shifted in the bed as her dream-state body reacted to the sensation throughout her body. She continued to watch as immediately after the energy ball struck, the Xeephin dealt the fatal stroke.

She stood by the bush and observed the ending battle from the small, troll-like creature's perspective. When the ball of light hit her, dream-state Tegan not only felt the energy rush, but she felt a wave of relief from the troll-creature's mind. She could feel what he felt for a moment.

Then she saw her capture and earthly ending. She didn't see and feel the darkness as she did when viewing through her physical eyes, but saw the battle from the troll's eyes. Then darkness, as though the being was no longer viewing the battle.

She felt the occhiolism of her life as she was aware of the smallness of her perspective in the grandness of the vast scope of the Universe. She felt that way in Phoenix after she realized that aliens in fact existed and were among us. But the aliens in the lab differed from the ones in Loveland.

In her mind's eye, she saw an image of her looking at what she felt was the universe, but it felt tiny from her perspective. The difference between what she thought she knew and what she just experienced was vastly different. Then she saw herself step back, only to realize she was observing from a keyhole that limited her range of vision. From that new position, life, purpose, and meaning took shape, concealed by the position of the keyhole in her prior view. There was more to what she experienced and saw. There was a universal plan, and she was an important, but small, part of the cycle. While she thought the creature hid in the bushes and didn't intervene, she now saw that it protected her. The ball of energy cast a powerful, protective spell over her that allowed her to come back to earth.

The images in her mind pulsated like a strobe light with a bright flash of light, then an almost still image. The process repeated. She saw herself surrounded by six higher beings all dressed in black, then a flash of bright light again. She saw another slow-moving image of the observed beings, then felt something grab her hand. She watched herself turn to see the being in blue take her hand and jerk her into his arms. She felt his embrace and saw another flash of light. Although she didn't know who this strange, faceless man was, or how he was with her, she felt peace and trust. She felt weightless, but was aware they were flying. Then a hard thud on her back. She felt that as well. Her vision was clouded, but as it cleared, her view from laying on the ground and looking up at a tree-covered area took shape. It was Loveland!

She recoiled in surprise as the next image in her mind was the hairy wildman's close-up face as he leaned in close to her face. She expected to jump, but she was not afraid. She saw the creature watch her for a moment, and then extend his hand. She could feel the little man's hand as it touched her head.

She felt a warmth as she saw a purple glow enter her head. Then her dream-avatar recognized her physical body open her eyes and saw the dense, purple light. As the flow dissipated, she could see the creature's face through the purple glow as it faded. He smiled. She saw her earthly body curl up in the fetal position as she regained consciousness.

The next image she saw was Kareem as he ran toward her still body. She felt his embrace as he comforted her and a wetness on her face as he cried in reaction to what happened. She saw Ty and Carson running in the background to check on her. She could feel their shock and disbelief at the horrific events that occurred in those final moments. The light flashed again. When the images returned, she was inside the ambulance. The lights flashed again, this time followed by darkness, then another flash. She saw herself in the hospital room. Then another flash. She saw an old man with a white beard wearing a winged helmet. He had a god-like presence, and a single word entered her mind. Odin. He raised and waved his hand over her head, and the visions ceased.

She remained in her dream, standing as she looked at the scene of a now empty Loveland hill. She was unaware that the little man was sitting next to her dream-avatar as they watched the finale together.

Shocked, the voice inside her head thought, That troll saved my life!

The Wildman turned toward Tegan's dream-avatar. Lucid dreamer Tegan noticed the motion and turned her head. She found herself face-to-face with two small red eyes from about a foot away.

Pukwudgie, replied Puddlesquat telepathically.

The dream-state observer screamed in unison with the now jerked awake three-dimensional Tegan on the couch.

6 Damsel In Distress

Tegan woke up just after 7:30 a.m. She took herself to the bedroom in the early morning hours and was fortunate to catch a few hours of rest after another sleepless night because of the now reoccurring dreams. She wasn't sure what she dreamed about after the Pukwudgie dream sequence, but she had an image of an enormous cat, a mountain lion or cougar stuck in her head.

She dismissed the visions as the result of being overstressed. In the past few months, she battled and lost to a large intergalactic frog-like creature, died, returned to life, and moved to a new city. She attempted to put those events behind her, but it was more difficult than she imagined. The aftereffects were regular sessions with Dr. Ollie, and now, recurring vivid dreams of weird images that involved bizarre creatures and scenes from her life. What did they mean? How were they connected?

Now that I'm up, she thought as she walked to the living room coffee table and turned on the laptop, *what the hell is a Pukwudgie?*

She opened her trusted search engine, entered the term, and received thousands of results that ranged from fantasy to cartoons to Native American lore. The physical traits showed the same creature and characteristics from her dreams: a troll-like creature that stood two to three feet in height, had grey skin, and with large fingers, noses, and coarse black hair. They were more commonly reported in Massachusetts within the Bridgewater Triangle area, but sightings also occurred throughout the Great Lakes region, including Illinois, Indiana, Michigan, Minnesota, New York, Ohio, Pennsylvania, and Wisconsin.

The results showed they are magical beings with an ability to glow, shapeshift into animals, push people off cliffs, and use weapons, such as small bows with poisoned tipped arrows or clubs. She recalled from her dream the creature carried a quiver of arrows on its back. Native American mythology believed if a human crossed the path of a Pukwudgie, they should avoid it as much as possible and should not interact with the being at all. One article described them as mischievous and dangerous to humans. Some believed they pushed people off cliffs, lured people to their deaths, and created fire. The ability to become invisible made sense to Tegan now that she saw the being in her dreams. She and Kareem both heard something in Loveland, but couldn't locate the source. Now she knew the creature observed from the shadows of the bushes.

They seem to be bad guys, she thought, *but this one helped me. I wonder why?*

The lore stated humans did not always consider Pukwudgies to be bad. At one time, they were friendly little people who helped the Native Wampanoag people. They always appreciated the Pukwudgies' help, even though most of their efforts to help often had the opposite intended effect. The Pukwudgie felt they were in competition for the Wampanoag's affection against the creation giant, Maushop. The Wampanoag felt blessed by Maushop and turned their attention to him, which caused the Pukwudgie to feel abandoned. As a result, they became mischievous and tormented the Wampanoag.

When the Wampanoag couldn't take anymore, they sought Maushop's wife, Granny Squannit. She directed Maushop to gather up as many Pukwudgies as possible. He shook them until they were confused and then flung them across New England. Some died, but others landed, regained their minds, and made their way back to their original area. When they returned, they were more violent than before and kidnapped children, burned homes or even entire villages to the ground, and chased many of the Wampanoag deep into the woods and killed them. Afterward, Granny Squannit once again instructed Maushop to get rid of the Pukwudgies. Instead, he sent his five sons to handle the job. However, the Pukwudgies were clever and lured the sons into deep grass and killed them with poisoned arrows.

The giant and his wife became enraged at the loss of their sons and set out to kill every Pukwudgie they could find. But many escaped and scattered throughout New England. The Pukwudgies again regrouped and tricked Maushop into the water, where they hit him with their poisoned arrows and killed him.

Wow, that's some shit, she thought to herself. *But before that, they were friendly. They enjoyed at least respect and acceptance of the Wampanoag people... they just wanted more. But why would it pick me?*

After reading multiple articles about the little *Wildman of the woods that vanishes*, she decided she wasn't interested in the strange little creature. It was just an odd dream, and that is all that it was. She turned on the television to distract her thoughts, but it was unsuccessful. She flipped through the channels and watched the images as they carouseled past. She noticed the movie *Narnia*, the animated movie *Madagascar*, and another channel aired a commercial that announced pre-sale tickets to the musical *The Lion King* were now on sale. Those images made her think about the most recent dream and the big cat that was a fleeting image in her mind as the details of her visions raced from memory.

Her level of interest increased, and felt compelled to determine the meaning behind the dreams. The details of her life over the past few months were a confused and out-of-place mess. She didn't used to have such vivid dreams. She couldn't help but notice everything in her life had changed over the past six months. Not only her dream habits, but her taste in music, clothing, and perfume changed. Now, her appearance also changed with the new hairstyle and tattoos.

Her mood also changed. Now she felt more confident and walked with a purpose where before she was shy and uncertain. Now she wasn't timid when she thought about nighttime investigations of mysterious entities or creatures, even if they were frogs or aliens. Months ago, before her death, she had a fear of frogs. What she experienced beneath the dam at Dreamy Draw caused trepidation that affected her for several months. She was no longer certain of her place in the universe, the purpose of life, or what happened after we die. Real existential shit that now no longer affected her. She was not afraid of death.

Been there, done that, she thought.

She knew there was more behind the curtain. Once we die, the physical body remained and withered away, but the soul journeyed on. She saw strange beings in her afterlife visions, but she had also seen her share of strange beings in her life prior to death. She wondered what else the veil of life concealed, and what else existed beyond it. The experience was a profound transcendental occurrence, where the boundaries between space, time, and normal perceptual awareness became blurred.

During her journey, she felt overwhelmingly positive emotions, including peace, unconditional love, and joy. Now death was no longer an obstacle or something she feared. Things she used to fear were no longer frightening because she knew what was on the other side and how it felt. She knew the universe had a message and a purpose for each of us. There were no coincidences. So maybe she should be interested in the strange little creature.

She recalled she first felt the uncertainty of her life and the disconnection with her prior habits after she left Guy Buffalo's Cincinnati casita and headed to Evansville. That crea… Pukwudgie… intervened in the fight. He protected her, at least somewhat. Like the origin of the Pukwudgie lore, maybe its intention was helpful, but had the opposite effect? She couldn't help but continue to wonder if they were harmful beings, why did this one attempt to save her? And how did she return to life?

She remembered from her dreams she saw the Pukwudgie a second time, but what happened in between? She felt confident the puzzle somehow involved the Pukwudgie, but what was its role in the universe's grand plan, and how did it involve her? In the past, when she had these types of questions and needed inner exploration to solve a problem, she found the gumption in one place, a bar.

Maybe I need a drink, she thought.

But where? She searched her mind and realized she had not had a beer since that afternoon at Arnold's in Ohio.

She pursed her lips and continued her thought. *I don't even know if I still like beer. So many things have changed. Maybe that has too?*

She flipped the television channel again and landed on an old cartoon where some dastardly villain was tying a petite young woman to the tracks as an oncoming train approached. Thankfully, the strong male hero arrived just in the nick of time to save her.

Tegan watched the scene with disgust as the hero escaped harm's way with the girl in his arms.

Damsel in distress. Stupid gender stereotype B.S., she said internally. *That trope has gotta go. Gender roles are dead.*

She returned the focus to her phone and opened the Untappd app for the first time in months.

"Let's see what's around here," she said aloud.

The app pulled up the results of nearby verified menus, within thirty miles of her location, and sorted by distance. She stared at the top result and gave an under-breath chuckle. The closest bar was just two miles away.

Damsel Brew Pub I guess it is, she reluctantly decided, as she continued to stare at the symbolic message.

It was a short drive to Damsel Brew Pub, and its parking lot wasn't full this time of day. She walked around the two-story brick building and found the entrance underneath the large black patio.

She stood outside for a moment. She stared at the door and felt her reflection staring back at her, like two gunslingers in the Old West. Putting hesitation aside, she walked closer and opened the door.

Inside, the bar was colorful with one wall that appeared to be brick and the others colored an avocado green. There were plenty of seats in the room, but she saw the bar was empty and approached it nostalgically.

"It's been a while," she said as she picked up the menu and reviewed it. A bartender approached, holding a glass of ice water.

"Need a minute?" he asked. "My name's Austin."

"Of course it is," she said.

"huh?"

"Nothing. It's been a while. I might need a few minutes." Tegan reviewed the menu and looked surprised. "You have absinthe? Isn't that illegal?"

"The Green Fairy? Not anymore, but it was. It's the stuff that inspired Vincent van Gogh's creativity," replied Austin.

"Don't you mean caused him to cut off his ear?" questioned Tegan.

"You take the good, you take the bad…" said Austin.

"Facts of life," responded Tegan. "Let me go with something light. It's been a while," she said as she returned her attention to the menu's options. After she read a few of the beers listed, she realized they were all the first name of a woman.

"Must be the damsels," she mumbled.

Austin walked over.

"Excuse me, did you say something? You ready to order?" clarified Austin.

"I was just noticing your beer selections, and… I'll have the Lizzy," she said.

"Coming right up," replied Austin. He turned his back for a moment, then turned back with a pint of the Berliner Weisse. "Raspberry shot?"

Tegan nodded in agreement and awaited the added pour. Austin handed it to her, and she held it up to her nose, closed her eyes, and inhaled.

Lemon, biscuit, and straw aroma, she thought. She smiled in anticipation and took a sip. It was an excellent beer with mild, sweet-tart lemon, sour lactic acid, and just enough hoppiness in the background. As she pulled away, her smile widened, and she sat the glass back on the bar.

"Still like beer."

"You like sours?" asked Austin.

"Yes, that's my favorite style. A Berliner Weisse, a gose, even sometimes I would enjoy those thicker sour fruited beers," she replied.

"Never could get into 'em myself. I prefer IPAs to most styles," he stated. "I've got something you might like. Do you like mead?"

"I've only had it a few times, but I recall liking it," she said.

"When you're ready for number two, let me know. I've got a mispour over here, and it's not my style. I hate to drain-pour it, so if you want it, it's yours," he concluded.

Tegan's eyes scanned the bar, and she felt comfortable again in the craft beer arena. Her eyes panned the interior of the bar and took it all in. To her left, she noticed a book on top of the local newspaper. She didn't see anyone leave it, but the cover caught her attention. It had what she thought was a geometric pattern, but after she picked it up, she noticed it was four women. The title read *Old Norse Women's Poetry: The Voices of Female Skalds by Sandra Ballif Straubhaar.*

Library of Medieval Women? Sounds badass, she thought.

She opened the book to discover that the Old Norse poetry was poetry written in the Old Norse Language.

Just like it says. How 'bout that? she thought.

The language was unfamiliar to her, and she could not read the content. As she continued to stare at the pages, her eyes refocused. Her view was blurry, but seconds later, her vision was clear. She glared at the page as she realized the words had changed. She could read and understand the message.

"What the hell? That's weird."

She drew back and placed the poetry book back on the bar top.

She finished the last sip of her beer, then glanced at her wristwatch before she decided she had time for one more. Before she could take the bartender up on his offer, a man walked up and asked the bartender for a recommendation.

"Do you like mead?" asked Austin.

"Yes, I love it. I have found little of it recently. I'd love to find a good one," said the new customer.

"Give this one a try. New Day Three Eyed Magpie. It's an Imperial Breakfast Magpie that's been aging for three years in an Angel's Envy bourbon barrel," offered Austin. He reached behind him and removed the honey wine from the counter. "On the house."

"Sounds great. I'll take it," the man said as he pulled a chair to the bar.

Tegan glanced down and wrinkled her face at the realization that she lost the free drink.

It's for the best not to accept an already poured drink, she thought. *Don't know where it's been.*

It did sound delicious, and she recalled she liked mead the few times she had ordered one in the past. When Austin came back around, he asked if she would like another drink.

"I'll have the Three Eyed Magpie too," she said.

"You just missed out on the free one," he replied.

"It's okay," she said as she sat her card on the table. "I have a job."

Austin nodded his head and asked, "Keep it open?"

While Austin walked to the end of the bar to pour the mead, Tegan's attention returned to the bar top. She noticed the newspaper that had been underneath the book showed a headline that began, *Unknown Creature*, and showed the left side of a photo. It drew her attention enough that she picked it up and unfolded the paper to read the full title. *Unknown Creature Stalks Gibson County.* She stared for a couple of seconds before she put it back on the bar top as Austin returned with the drink. "Just in time," she said.

She picked up the glass and held it to her nose to take a quick inhale. She detected notes of espresso.

A small amount. Must be some powerful stuff, she thought.

She sipped from the glass and picked up the sweetness from the wildflower honey and grape, but the espresso balanced it and kept it from being too sweet. She reviewed the menu, and it surprised her to see the alcohol percentage was twenty-point-five percent. The espresso must also mask the alcohol, she concluded. She recognized it had the potential to sneak up on one.

"It's thick and sweet and has a high ABV, but it's smooth despite that," Austin said. "Let me know if you need anything else," he said before heading to the end of the bar to wash glasses and wipe down the bar top.

She nodded and took another small sip. Suddenly, she felt a jolt and visions invaded her mind again. She saw the image of the big cat she saw in her dreams last night, then the image of the newspaper in front of her. The pictures continued to flood her mind with powerful messages.

The big cat in her dreams is the same unknown creature stalking Gibson County, she thought. *Why am I dreaming about this animal?* she wondered.

She hadn't been to Gibson County but once or twice during her time in Indiana, even though it was only thirty minutes away from her apartment. She knew it was more rural than where she lived, with a lot of trees and farms where a cat, even an enormous cat like a mountain lion, might be difficult to locate.

I don't even know where to begin, she thought.

Then another image entered her head. She saw a gray barn near a thick wood. Across a small driveway, she saw a beige brick house with a tall flagpole in the yard. Then she observed the animal prowling the area behind the barn, as it emerged out of the woods near dusk.

Concentrate, she heard in her head. Startled by the invasive thought, she glanced around the bar, but there was no one around her. She closed her eyes and tried to focus on the images.

Something clicked, and the answer appeared in her mind. *Owensville* and the number *675 South*.

She looked at the drink and wondered why these visions happened. The drink was excellent, and she liked it. It was sweeter than the sour beers she used to drink, but she enjoyed it. She looked around the bar once again, but noticed only a few customers: the man who absconded the free drink and settled a few seats away from her, and another guy to her left who was busy looking at his cell phone.

Other than them, the only other patrons at the bar were two guys on the far side of the bar: a tall, skinny man wearing a black hoodie and, to his right, a male little person with a thick, bushy black beard. Both men were occupied with other things. The taller man had his hood up, his head down, and appeared to be listening to music. The little person focused on the television. She again picked up the newspaper and skimmed the article, looking for more information.

Hello, Tegan, she heard within her head.

It caused her to put the newspaper down and look up once again. Once again, she scanned the brewery's patrons. When her attention returned to the hooded man and little person, she paused. The man's head remained lowered, but she thought she detected a faint blue glow from under his hood.

I know you can hear me, said the voice inside her head.

Her focus remained on the hooded man. He surprised her, but she felt unafraid.

How can I hear you? she wondered internally.

Marcus Aralias said that death smiles at every man, but he can only smile back, the hooded man replied telepathically. *But you did more than that, didn't you? You smashed through it and got a second chance.*

I have, but I don't know how, and everything feels different, she answered mentally.

Have you talked to others about your experiences? On the hill in Loveland? he asked

She continued to stare at the duo but didn't feel threatened. She felt at peace despite the strange internal conversation. She didn't answer.

Don't be hesitant. It's not the first time you have experienced telepathy. Ingrid Cole in Vermont, the beings in the white light after Loveland… and my friend Puddlesquat here visits your dreams, said the hooded man without looking up.

I gave up speaking to people about my experiences in Loveland. Other than Dr. Ollie, she replied. *At first, I tried, but it was difficult. A sense of exulansis overcame me and stopped trying.*

Perhaps we can offer some answers, replied the man. *My name is Santiago Torres, and this is my Pukwudgie companion, Puddlesquat.*

We've met, she replied. Puddlesquat acknowledged with a wave of his large hand. *And what are you?*

Just a man. A bus boy from Chile, though some call me a necromancer, he added.

Necromancer? Did you have anything to do with my death? she asked.

Death? No. Rebirth? Yes. Puddlesquat did most of the work, but I played a part, he responded.

Austin returned to Tegan and saw her sitting without a drink. "Can I get you another?"

"Just water right now," she stated, before returning to her conversation with the hooded man.

What happened in Loveland? I remember we were investigating and heard what sounded like footprints in the fallen leaves, but we saw nothing. The past few nights in my dreams, I relived that scene and saw your friend under the bushes, she said.

He was there and knew the outcome before it happened, Santiago replied. *The energy you felt was a protection spell he cast. He knew the Xeephines would defeat you, but he could provide comfort and mark you for retrieval.*

Retrieval? she asked.

That's where I come in, answered Santiago. *I've learned skills that involve*

astral projection. Puddlesquat watched as the battle unfolded. As soon as the Xeephin engulfed you, he told me to retrieve you. I projected to the astral plane. There are thousands of beings, as well as humans, but I could locate you thanks to Puddlesquat's spell.

In my dreams and earlier with Dr. Ollie under hypnosis, I saw a blue light, and I felt a jerk and a thud, she replied.

I can return people from the astral plane by grabbing them and jumping back to earth, Santiago stated. *You were among the beings in the light. I grabbed your hand and embraced you, then returned to Loveland after your friend Kareem shot the visitor.*

The doctors said I died in the ambulance on the way to the hospital, she replied.

Doctors are often wrong with near-death experiences and astral projection, answered Santiago. *It took some time for your body to accept the magic. Your vitals dipped on the way to the hospital. Think of it as a reboot. The doctor didn't read the charts correctly because most don't understand magic.*

What happened when you returned me to Loveland? she asked.

The Xeephin exploded from Kareem's weapon and

your body, still dead, fell to the ground. Puddlesquat was invisible to your friends. He could move in and touch your head, invoking a purple healing light that not only revived you to life, but transferred his powers to you. Next, Kareem ran to comfort you until the medics arrived. You passed out twice on the way to the hospital, but were out of danger by the morning, Santiago explained.

In my dreams, I saw the purple light and his face through it, she said.

You experienced everything as it happened, but your mind could not process it, so your brain blocked it out. In meditation or through dreams, you can see the truth, he added.

You mentioned powers. What powers? And why would he give powers to me, or save me, for that matter? I read Pukwudgies are mischievous and mean, she replied.

Puddlesquat shot her a displeased facial expression from across the bar.

They weren't always. There was a time when they were friends with humans and loyal to each other. What do you know about your grandmother? Santiago asked.

My grandmother? Not much. I knew her before she died, but I always thought of her as kind, confident, and a bit… eccentric, Tegan recalled.

And powerful, added Santiago.

Wait, you knew her? Have you seen her on the astral plane?

I have not yet seen her, nor did I know her. But Puddlesquat did, replied Santiago.

He did?

She was indeed powerful, as were all her kind, he stated.

Her kind? What kind is that?

The Valkyrie.

Valkyrie? I thought those were things of legend, said Tegan.

You should know by now that every legend contains some truth. In the olden days, they worked with Odin.

Odin? I thought I saw his image in my dream last night, added Tegan.

Odin could see the future and commune with spirits and the dead. He was also a shapeshifter who could take the form of snakes, eagles, and other powerful creatures. Odin spoke in poetic verse and had the power to bewitch humans into committing deeds outside their character. The Valkyrie shared many of those powers. They have the power to give victory to one of the warring sides, an ability encapsulated in the description of a battle as the Judgement of Gondul. It's a metaphor which compares the clash of two armies to a court where both sides litigate, but a judge, the Valkyrie, gives only one party victory. They can move around unseen. They can take the form of birds or animals. Many fly with wings.

My grandmother had these powers? she asked.

Yes, and thanks to her, so does Puddlesquat, he added. *Your Grandma was a Valkyrie and saved the Pukwudgies by protecting them and choosing them victorious in battle over an entity in the Pine Barrens,* Santiago stated.

Pine Barrens? New Jersey? I read the Pukwudgies lived in Massachusetts and scattered throughout New England by Maushop.

That's correct. With your grandmother banishing the Jersey Devil and choosing the Pukwudgies as the victors in the battle, this act created a debt the Pukwudgies pledged to repay.

The Jersey Devil? Wait, wasn't that creature first spotted in the 1700s? My grandmother wasn't that old, added Tegan.

Your grandmother could defeat age, that's why modern-day Valkyries all have youthful appearances. She banished the Jersey Devil in 1736, but it returned in the early 1900s. She defeated it once more in the winter of 1911. After you were born, she decided it was time to move on from this plane of existence, stated Santiago.

This is all a lot to take in, replied Tegan. *So many questions. What powers did Puddlesquat grant me?*

Obviously, telepathy, began Santiago. *Foresight and the ability to determine the victors in battle, the ability to shapeshift into birds or other winged animals. They often saw Valkyries from above the battlefield, hence their ability to fly. They were well-known for serving and brewing mead, and as you experienced earlier, mead allows you the ability to receive visions. And like Odin, you can read Old Norse and write poetry.*

This old book beside me on the bar top is an Old Norse book of poetry. When I picked it up earlier, it took a moment for my eyes to see it, but I could read and understand it. It was like the words adjusted and I could see it as plain as the English in the newspaper below it, Tegan revealed.

Your new look, the tattoo, the hairstyle, and the strange feelings of confidence reflect a modern-day Valkyrie, he said. *Especially once you get the Ouroboros with the Tree of Life. Those are Norse symbols.*

What do modern-day Valkyries… like me… do? asked Tegan.

A modern-day Valkyrie is a woman who is an everyday warrior. Whether it's battling demons in the past, in the mind, or life events and stress, she's a shield-maiden through and through. Strong and vulnerable. She's been wounded, yet she lives and thrives. There are three practices shield-maidens follow to allow them to be at their best, he said.

Based on my experiences, my death, and my return trip, it sounds like I fit the description, she stated.

Yes, and you can continue to grow by learning more, he replied.

What are these three things?

Foremost, help others. You have the foresight to see inside them, know their deepest secrets and desires, help them advance to the next stage of their development, and ascend to the fifth dimension. Second, practice visualization. It allows you the capability to remote view a location and communicate with humans, animals, and other beings. Third, recharge your emotions and abilities. Get outside and take a forest bath, he stated.

Forest bath? Like in a lake? she enquired.

Not literally. Enjoyment of the scenery and being in nature tranquilizes the mind. It's a refreshing reset. Spend time in the forested areas to enhance health, wellness, and happiness. Walk in the woods and be mindful of your environment. It's not about taking an exhausting hike or walking in a noisy city park, but to connect with the forest and open yourself, emotionally and spiritually, to enhance your health and well-being. It's called Shinrin Yoku, he explained. *You, like other modern Valkyries, are both at once a lioness, but also soft and sensual as silk. You are fearless. Why should fear or death affect you? You have faced and defeated both. You are associated with strength and protection. You are independent, but function well with a team as a protector and a kick-ass woman that takes no shit.*

Santiago and Puddlesquat stood and headed toward the door.

Here's a gift to mark your new journey, he stated as he paused beside her and placed a small blue and silver piece of jewelry on the bar top, then continued to walk toward the bar's door. As he left the room, he continued the telepathic conversation.

This is a Lagertha shield bracelet. She was a Viking shield-maiden and ruler of what is now Norway. With her unmatched spirit and courage, she fought the bravest men. She wore her hair loose over her shoulders and it flowed down her back, betraying the fact she was a woman. Wear it as a reminder that you are strong and fearless.

What do I do now? asked Tegan.

Help the people of Owensville and stop the beast that stalks them, he said.

The duo left the brewery and passed through the door without it being opened, showing Tegan both were in their astral forms, even though they appeared to her as humans.

7 Shinrin-Yoku

After Santiago and Puddlesquat left the brewery, Tegan felt overwhelmed by the new information they provided. She already knew she had died in Loveland and somehow returned. The doctors said it happened on the way to the hospital and the medical staff revived her, but now she knew it was because of these two strange beings. Although Santiago was a normal man, his behavior and his skills were extraordinary.

She learned her grandmother was a Valkyrie and saved the Pukwudgies in a battle against the Jersey Devil in the 1700s. That would have been enough to rock her world before, but now she accepted it with calmness. She believed Santiago's accounts because she saw him and Puddlesquat in her dreams over the past several nights. She didn't know what the dreams meant then, but now she had a better understanding.

Puddlesquat received the powers of the Valkyrie by her grandmother and like her, he can foreshadow and choose the victor in battles. He didn't stop her death at the hands of the Xeephines, but he chose her to survive after defeat. She had seen the blue aura of Santiago and the purple light from Puddlesquat and watched her battle from a new perspective in her dreams. She and Kareem heard unseen footsteps on the Loveland hill, but this time, she could see Puddlesquat there all along.

Despite the crazy tale that Santiago retrieved her from the astral plane and Puddlesquat not only brought her back to life, but instilled the powers of the Valkyrie within her, her dreams, and now her gut feeling, told her the tale was true. She had felt differently since she moved to Evansville, almost felt like a different person. She experienced visions when she drank mead. It was something she hadn't experienced previously with the drink. Not to mention, she just had an entire telepathic conversation with a man from across the bar.

She knew things differed from before, and she accepted it. Her discovery of the alien ship and the files of cryptids in Phoenix shook her.

The experience in Loveland took it to another level, but this time she felt comfortable and confident with what would have been an earth-shattering paradigm shift. Now she wanted to learn more.

Santiago told her there were three important parts of being a modern-day Valkyrie: helping others see and get to their true path, visualization and communication with humans and animals, and a forest bath. She had to learn more about what that last element meant.

She was down with the first element. Helping people was what she knew and practiced as a therapist. She knew by practicing empathy for others, even when we sometimes feel they don't deserve it, was empowering. As a kid, she helped her mom with her siblings as much as needed. In Austin, she helped the team with the investigations of mysterious creatures, which also helped the people of the local communities. When the team solved mysteries, she knew it helped put the community at ease and saved lives.

The second element she knew helped the mind. She understood that through visualization, one could reprogram the brain. The power of positivity and the ability to picture herself with certain skills and attributes could help improve those skills. Science had proven that visualization could develop and help improve those skills. Plus, she could see in other ways now. She could get a visual image and the location of the animal in Gibson County, and was ready once again to help the people of a small community who felt threatened by an unknown creature.

Including the forest bath surprised her. She knew Valkyries were Norse, but the name Santiago called it, Shinrin Yoku, sounded Japanese. She turned to her phone to learn more about the concept and found it involved a clear mind while being surrounded by nature. As a result, it enhanced the health, wellness, and happiness of the practitioner. It wasn't physical exertion in the woods, but rather a comfortable walk in nature and being mindful of the environment.

She spent a lot of time in nature when the team investigated, but that was always a stressful experience, the opposite of what a forest bath provided. Mindfulness involved a walk along a path, an embrace of the aromas from the trees and shrubs, the relaxation created by the sound of running water, the tactile sensation caused by the touch of the trees, and connecting with nature on another level. Valkyries possessed superhuman strength and foresight. The connection to nature helped recharge both mind and body to prepare them for battle.

She read Valkyries could use their magical powers to bring selected fallen heroes back to life. This followed the experience she had with Puddlesquat, who repaid the debt to her grandmother for the help she gave his people.

She knew about the concept of grounding and how positive energy entered one's body through the soles of their bare feet in contact with the grass, but the concept of forest bathing was new to her. She thought back to her time at the bar in Austin, not the craft beer bars, but the Meditation Bar. She was a new member there before her trip to Loveland but had committed to herself to discover who she was, and to become the type of person she desired to be. Then she died and now everything was confusing. She felt different, she looked different, and she learned more about the world she didn't know than she ever expected. That seemed to happen a lot.

The field of cryptozoology blew what she knew of the world out of sight. Then the discovery of aliens in Phoenix expanded that to depths she didn't think could be further from her reality. But after her death, rebirth, and meeting with Santiago and Puddlesquat. Now she wasn't sure what to believe. She was no longer afraid, and more willing to accept challenges to her beliefs, but it was still a lot to take in.

Ready to test out the process before she began her journey to Owensville, she drove to Green River State Forest. It was just sixteen miles from Evansville and provided a peaceful retreat to implement the process of the forest bath.

She arrived at the parking lot, left the car, and entered the forest with an anticipation. She wasn't sure why, but she was excited. The park was in Kentucky, but close to home. It was one of the lushest forests in the area and contained just under eleven hundred square acres, just a few miles outside of Henderson. It contained tree and lakes but was also open to the public for many recreational uses.

She found a spot near the beige trailer that served as the visitor's center off Tscharner Road and walked a trail that led deep into the woods. As she walked, she noticed every shade of green that she could imagine, every shape and size of leaf that she could think of. She noticed the trees with smooth bark, rough bark, peeling bark, rotting bark… the smell of pine trees mixed with the distinct aroma of fetid earth. The sound of small animals rustled in the leaves as they scurried under the thick ferns and over the thousands of brittle branches and twigs… the constant sound of a breeze that swayed the trees with its caress… birds that twittered and flew from tree to tree. She took it all in as she continued to search for a meditation spot.

The weather was mild over the past few days. Rays of mellow sunlight filtered through the verdurous canopy, penetrated through the leaves, and cast an unearthly green–gold luminescence over the ground, which made the weather even more manageable. She looked around the path and located a spot that overlooked a small pond within the forest. Wet from the late winter rainfall, the ground was dark and damp. The fallen curled brown leaves were half-embedded in it, trampled by the occasional dog walker. Its form crisply remembered the small prints of rodents and birds.

Tegan brushed aside the leaves and sat in a cross-legged position and closed her eyes. She focused with the intention of mindfulness. She took in her surroundings and fought off negative thoughts such as the growing level of stress in the world and how modern society was more cut off from nature. Many people feared being outdoors and wouldn't go out in nature because they were uncomfortable. But she knew humans were meant to be in nature. She theorized there was a connection between the disconnection from nature and the increased feelings of stress and depression.

She read online during her research that one who practiced Shinrin Yoku should bring an offering. She reached into her purse and removed a small leather pouch that contained tobacco and a leaf from a butternut tree. She laid them down in the tall grass and again closed her eyes as she drifted further into a deeper meditative state. Tegan felt connected to beings from other dimensions who live with us. Even though they are around, to sense we must connect with nature. She focused her mind and approached with respect. Soon she observed the feeling that she was being watched.

Although she didn't see them visually prior to her meditation session, she sensed the other beings nearby. First birds and nearby forest animals, but she could filter out noise and focus on a concise reading.

As she fine-tuned her surroundings, she noticed the thoughts of another beast. A beast too large for what most people accepted to live there.

She received a mental image of a bipedal being between seven-and-a-half and eight feet tall and weighed over seven hundred pounds.

The beast told her telepathically it hid from people and searched for food, but it had become more difficult to remain hidden as human expansion continued relentlessly.

What's your name? she asked telepathically.

My name is Allutus, he returned mentally. Your scientists call me Gigantopithecus Ukohhaii, and locals call me The Spottsville Monster, he replied. He lowered his head and shoulders from his hidden spot in the trees as he thought about the name. Although Tegan didn't see it visually, she sensed a change in his emotions.

I'm sorry, Tegan returned.

I'm not a monster, I'm just trying to survive as my habitat shrinks, he responded. I remained hidden for many years, but one day in the lonely bottom lands of Western Kentucky, I ran into a woman off what you call Mound Ridge Road. She screamed, Monster! And word spread. People stopped coming to the woods because they heard of a frightening monster that was said to dwell in the foreboding forests. I'm glad fewer humans came, but still… The stigma is hurtful.

I understand, Tegan acknowledged. I don't think you're a monster. I can sense your soul, she said telepathically.

Allutus stepped from the coverage of the trees to stand behind Tegan and observe, but she remained peaceful with her eyes closed, not noticing the physical creature behind her. The telepathic image and soul assessment was sufficient.

She remained seated and searched deep inside herself to connect to the nature and earth, the connection to the Japanese Shinrin Yoku through its relationship to Nordic shamanism and forest therapy. Allutus stepped back into the volume of leaves of the forest and once again disappeared.

Thank you for your kindness, he thought. Good luck on your journey.

Tegan continued to search the depths of her soul and strengthen the connection to her surroundings. Soon, she felt it. An embrace without judgment, caressing her with its beautiful sounds and smells. Feelings of power and support washed over her. She could visualize herself leaving the fuss of a busy life and smooth asphalted roads behind and being greeted with peaceful and fragrant nature. Now, there was no need to perform, no need to always try to be perfect. She could be just the way she was and just be there.

She felt a warm wave engulf her, and she felt powerful and confident enough to head to Owensville and search for this mysterious beast stalking the locals. Her mind returned to Allutus and how the locals misjudged his nature and his intentions. She pondered if that was the case in Gibson County as well? She would soon find out.

She smiled, thinking of the possibilities. She reached into her purse once again and removed a small handmade corn doll. She propped it up against the trunk of a nearby tree and left it as a gift to the forest and its beings as a symbol of gratitude for showing her the answers to her questions. As she left it as an offering, she could sense she was still being watched. She stood up and walked toward the car, certain of her next step in her journey.

8 The Iron Horse

From Green River State Forest, it was less than an hour's drive on U.S. Route 41 to Owensville. Tegan remembered Carson stating in one of their first adventures that if you wanted to find out what's happening in a community, stop by the local tavern. Adjusting her route, she turned left onto Indiana State Road 168 and turned left onto North West Street in the Town of Fort Branch, just seven miles short of Owensville.

Since the earliest days of settlers in the New World, beer and taverns were a part of the attitudes, customs, and landscape that became the fabric of America. The whispers of revolution in Colonial America began in local taverns. They were staples in the social, political, and travel lives of colonial citizens very early in this country's existence. Today, taverns, local bars, and breweries continue to provide spaces to meet and discuss local happenings, gossip, social gatherings, political planning, and destinations for travelers. If there was an unknown creature stalking the locals in this county, the regulars of the local watering hole would know about it.

She found a small parking area at the crossroads of West Vine and North McCreary, and just across the street, a weathered gray barn near the railroad tracks. The exterior signage read *Iron Horse Bar and Grill.* The line of motorcycles in front of the building signaled the potential for colorful characters and an entertaining customer base.

As she approached the door, her stomach rumbled, a sign her legendary appetite was alive and well. She scanned the area once inside. The long wooden bar, the pool tables, and an oversized Harley Davidson lamp anchored above the table caused the bar to seem familiar and reminded her of a few dive bars around Austin. Its clientele appeared to be locals who had lived in the area most of their lives. Exactly what Tegan had hoped to find.

She walked further into the dimly lit interior and found an empty spot in the middle of the bar. The other customers took notice and watched the unfamiliar woman take a seat. A middle-aged man with his brown hair pulled back into a ponytail approached and slid a paper menu toward her.

"Water while you look over the menu?" asked the bartender.

"Yes, please," she said as she looked down and scanned both the menu in front of her and the men who sat around the bar. A man at the end of the bar, who also wore his gray hair in a ponytail, took a long drag on his Winston cigarette, and sighed, which caused the smoke to billow out of his nose and mouth. He picked up the highball glass that held a double shot of whiskey, three fingers wide. He took an extended sip before he placed it down and took another puff of the cigarette. She could tell he spent a lot of time in the sun. His skin looked like melted pennies and hadn't seen a drop of lotion in years, if ever. He wore a black leather jacket that depicted his motorcycle club, the Grave Cats. Its image was a black cat perched on top of a tombstone under a full moon.

Two men between Tegan and the man in the corner dropped a couple of twenties on the bar and left. Tegan scooted closer to the man as the bartender returned with the water.

"You ready to order?" he asked.

Since living in Indiana the past couple of months, she tried the traditional sandwich of Indiana, a handmade, breaded tenderloin sandwich. She didn't see any reason to deviate from that now.

"Triple Jack, neat," she said.

It showed she was more than just a craft beer drinker and had no problem hanging with the boys. The order took the bartender a bit by surprise as he nodded and stepped back.

"Comin' right up."

She knew she passed the first test. Bikers respect bartenders. The acknowledgement showed the bartender thought she was all right, which meant the bikers would assume she was okay too. She knew if the bartender can't stand someone, the clientele would sense that too.

She also knew how to scan the room and read patches. The patches on a biker's jacket tell a story about what club the wearer's part of, whether it's a Motorcycle Club or Riding Club, what city he's from, what territory his club claimed, and whether he was a prospect or a member. She could tell if there were multiple clubs present. Even though she didn't have an intimate knowledge of which clubs were friendly and which hated each other's guts, she at least felt comfortable enough to be aware of the potential for trouble.

"Haven't seen you around here before," said the man with a raspy voice.

"Nope. Just passing through."

"To where?" replied the man, just before he took another extended inhale on his Winston.

"Owensville," she said.

"Just down the road a piece. Whatcha looking for there?"

"Have you heard anything about a strange creature in town? Saw a story in the paper the other day about it," she said.

"I heard something," he said. "Maybe seen something too."

"What did you see?" she asked as she took a sip of the smooth, smoky, and sweet drink before her.

"Something I've never seen before, but my Daddy talked about it when I was a kid," he admitted.

"How do you know it was the same thing?" she asked.

"He described it similar to a mountain lion, but larger."

"There aren't any mountain lions in Indiana," Tegan responded.

"So they say," the man replied.

"When did your dad see it?" she asked.

"Around 1935," he replied. "There were several sightings of an enormous cat roaming the countryside. It wasn't until November when a local named J. Oscar Hunt saw from his window this creature prowling around the barn on his property. He had seen it for weeks and feared the creature would kill the pigs he raised. One night, he heard some commotion in the barn and ran outside in his pajamas with his shotgun clutched in his fist. It was dark and he couldn't get a clear look at it, but he knew what it was and had to act. Aiming into the darkness, he fired several shots at the thing," replied the man.

"Did he kill it?" Tegan asked.

"Don't know. He didn't find a body, so he must have missed. Dad grew up just down the road from the Hunt's place.

"Did they see it again?"

"No. Never did. Oscar's wife talked about tracks they found around the house and near the barn."

"What type of tracks?" asked Tegan.

"She didn't describe them other than they were big. She said you could put your fists in them," he added.

"That must have been a large animal," responded Tegan.

"Other strange thing was there were six tracks," he replied.

"Six tracks?"

"This creature had six legs. They also claimed a loud roar had woken them up several nights in a row, like it was still stalking the house," he reported.

"I didn't think mountain lions roared," said Tegan.

"When they talked about it, they said it sounded like a lion, but had no proof. Hunt and other area farmers launched search parties and set traps. They even sprinkled meat around the woods, but the beast never took the bait. It didn't even mess with Hunt's livestock. They came to call it the Gibson County Beast. That was the last they saw of it, that I know of. Until recently," he said.

"Where did you encounter this animal?" she asked.

"Close over'ta Owensville, now that you mention it," the man replied. "I was riding with my buddy, Jerry, along 168. Close to the city limits. Just past the church."

"Did Jerry see it too?"

"Hell yeah, ran right across the street in front of us. He had to swerve to keep from hitting it, and swerving on these bikes isn't something it's designed to do," he replied.

"Do you think I could talk to Jerry?" Tegan asked.

"Probably could make that happen," said the man. "But he doesn't care too much for strangers, so I don't know what he'll say."

"I can take care of myself," she added.

Staring at her for a moment, the man nodded.

"I'll call him up tonight. Give me your number."

She grabbed a napkin and a pen from the bar top in front of the vacated seat, scrawled her number on it, and then pushed it toward the man.

"Did I hear you say something about a creature?" asked another man a couple of seats down.

"Yes. You see anything out of the ordinary around the area?" Tegan asked.

"Matter of fact, my buddy Daryl told me yesterday about something he saw near his property," replied Matt, another biker with a black Vietnam Veteran ball cap and a long gray beard.

"What did he say?"

"He lives out off of 775 West and said he saw a large animal around the woods and ponds in the area. He got a bit of a firsthand glimpse of it one night."

"Did he recognize it?" Tegan asked.

"Not really. He said it was a cat, but it was nearing dark. Only thing he could see for sure was the eyes. He said it had eyes that shined in the dark. Eyes that are bright and yellow," replied Matt.

"Anything else that stood out?"

"He just mentioned its size. Bigger than any cat he ever saw," answered Matt. "He also thought it had six legs, but wasn't sure he wasn't seeing things in the dark."

"Six legs? He's sure it was a cat? Maybe a bear or something?" asked Tegan. "I don't know any mammals that have six legs."

"He said it was a cat from the way it walked. He found tracks that were broad enough to be a bear, but they were feline. He got some of his buddies to come out and form a search party with guns and dogs. They followed the tracks a good way along the roads and across fields, but lost the tracks around the ponds. They went out last Saturday but found nothing. Monday, they heard a loud sound out in the woods about a quarter mile west of town," added Matt.

"What kind of noise?"

"A roar like a massive cat. We're talking lion or tiger. Or maybe it was a Bigfoot, he thought," added Matt sarcastically.

"Bigfoot?" Tegan questioned.

"Yeah, he's inta those kinds of shows. I told him there's no Bigfoot out here," dismissed Matt.

"You never know. There are a lot of strange animals out there waiting to be discovered," replied Tegan.

"I don't believe that stuff," said Matt. "Do you?"

"I've seen some things myself," Tegan said as she took another drink. "Some shit you wouldn't believe."

"They went out again on Tuesday and saw more tracks, but no sign of the animal. The papers picked up on the story, but there wasn't much to go on until Wednesday."

"What happened Wednesday?" asked Tegan.

"They ran another story about Miss Ellie Orr, a widow just north of town. Talk to her. I think she was the last to see it," replied Matt.

"Do you know her number?"

"Not rightly, but she's up Route 65 out by the old coal mine. Off County Road 675 South. Not too far from Daryl. Just her farm and a couple of houses out there," replied Matt.

"675? I saw that number in a dream. I can find it," Tegan replied. "Have your guy call me tonight and I will meet with him tomorrow. Thanks for your time. You've been a big help in getting more information on this creature," she said as she stood, threw cash down on the bar, and left.

9 Don't Lose Your Head

The moon was overhead as night enveloped Owensville and the hills that surrounded Ellie Orr's farm. The skies were clear and the temperature much already colder than it had been in recent days, and the forecast called for it to drop to a low of eight degrees. There were few clouds, but snow fell from those that were present. As the night progressed, the snow increased in intensity.

The wind blew through the empty branches of trees on a hill near the back of the north pasture. The sound increased as the wind reached seventeen miles per hour. It blew loose leaves and twigs across the ground, while the branches in the trees danced. One thing that did not increase in volume, in fact it remained silent, was a dark shadow as it slunk down the side of the hill.

The shadow emerged from the wood line. It was a large feline that, although dark tan during the day, was cloaked in black except for its bright yellow eyes. Walking down the side of the hill to the edge of the fence, it continued. Even without the aid of a nearby fallen tree just a few feet away, the beast leaped over the fence in a single bound.

Despite the height and the power of the creature's six muscular legs, it landed on the other side in the snowy pasture. It lowered itself close to the ground, and advanced with short, quick movements. The stealthy animal approached the crowd of hogs that remained unaware of the imminent danger.

Through the pasture, it prowled past larger hogs unnoticed. As it drew closer, the animals panicked as the large predator was within their perimeter. Many hogs began to run and squeal as they raced past the creature who did not react to them. It already locked its sights onto a target inside. The sudden, loud sound from the terrified hogs awakened Miss Ellie and caused her to sit up and then turn on the lamp beside her bed.

The creature continued its slow pursuit toward the front of the pen, where it cornered a weaner hog. Trapped between the feed trough and the massive animal that blocked its path, the pig had nowhere to run. It attempted to go left, but stopped as the beast moved in the same direction. Then toward the right, but once again, its intentions were thwarted. Unable to get past the snarling beast, it backed into the corner. From there, it could only shrink down in terror as it realized the end was near.

The creature raised up on its two hind legs, then came down on the hog. It used its front and middle claws to hold the pig in place, and its massive jaws to break the bones of its prey. The beast attacked the young hog at its neck until the smaller animal had no fight remaining. Victorious, it grabbed the fallen victim by the neck and drug its lifeless body through the pasture into a clearing near the back. Out of sight from Miss Ellie's frantic eyes, the cat grabbed its meal by the gullet and feasted as it ripped its prey and ate its organs.

The other animals stayed untouched in the furthest corner of the pasture, as the cat was uninterested in them after it already had satisfied its hunger for the night.

Tegan sat in the bed of her apartment while she watched soccer on ESPN. Her cellphone rang, which caused her to put the bowl of butter brickle ice cream on the nightstand.

"Hello?" she asked to the unknown caller.

"It's Daryl. Matt told me to call you."

"Hello, Daryl. Your friend told me about a mysterious six-legged animal saw," stated Tegan.

"Yeah, but what Matt don't know…. is that wasn't my first time seeing it.

"It wasn't?"

"No, I've seen it before. But I don't want to say too much on the phone," he said. "They're listening."

"Who is listening?"

He didn't answer the question. "I saw it once before. I can only talk in person.

"Okay, are you available tomorrow?" he asked.

"Yes, just say when and where."

"I'm going to meet up with a friend at the Barley & Barrel in Princeton. Be there at eleven thirty," he said as he hung up the phone.

10 Rising From The Dirt Like A Growing Vegetable

It was half-past eleven when Tegan pulled into the craft beer bar in Princeton, Indiana, precisely the time and location she and Daryl agreed upon last night when they spoke. He didn't want to give many details over the phone, fearful someone may be listening to the conversation. He didn't respond when Tegan asked him who would be listening, but she recalled Matt said his friend held on to some views that were maybe a bit in the outer realm. Was Bigfoot in the outer realm? After what she experienced first-hand over the past few years, she wasn't sure where the outer realm was anymore. Even though the brief conversation was over the phone, she sensed he had a good heart and had more information that would help her with the investigation.

The Barley & Barrel had preparations underway as it approached its second anniversary. It offered patrons a spacious facility to enjoy craft beer on tap, as well as a large variety of cans and bottles from around the United States, but also with a few international options. Beer from around the Hoosier State made up one entire cooler and was the most popular choice among customers.

A large twenty-eight tap area for draft pours sat in the center of a large room with wooden flooring. A bricked wall flanked it on either side and boasted three large screen televisions atop four coolers for bottles and cans. The walls faced inward and came together at a one-hundred-degree angle, with thirteen chairs along the stainless-steel bar. The room contained several wooden high-top tables between the bar and the front door.

Four lengthy, vinyl-covered booths with stainless tables centered within their boundaries sat along the side of the back wall. Tegan knew she was meeting with two guys and glanced at the booths as she walked up to the bar. It appeared as if her guests had not yet arrived. She requested three menus from the bartender as she informed him she expected two others to join her. He acknowledged her request as she took a seat at one of the empty booths.

Booths are comfortable, allow more space to eat while enjoying a few beers, and provide a certain level of privacy that increases the ability to discuss things the public may not be ready to hear. According to the newspapers, the locals were already up in arms because of the multiple sightings of an unknown creature, but Tegan felt they didn't need to risk the shock to those who may not have seen the articles.

She felt a slight tingling sensation cascade over her head as she scanned the other seats around the bar and central area. There were a few other guests at the bar, a couple at a table in the middle, but she could not get a visual from the other booths. She could see customers in booths as she walked into the bar, but given her height, she could not see above the booths to know when someone entered or left the bar.

She paused as she studied everyone within eyesight. She felt nothing that stood out about them as she attempted to examine their minds and souls. The tingling seemed to generate from a nearby source, but she couldn't get a reading on who it was or from where. It was as though the source had a protective ability to shield itself from her senses. Just then, a tall, muscular man in a denim vest reading *Grave Cats* interrupted her thoughts. He eclipsed the light as he approached her booth.

"Looks like you found the place," Daryl said as he took a seat opposite Tegan and slid to the left to allow his friend to take a seat. "This here's Cody."

"Hey there. Cody," said the man with an extended hand, combed red hair, black glasses, and an eager smile.

"Nice to meet you," she said as she recognized the vast differences between the two men. "This is a cool place. Daryl said you guys hang out here a lot?"

"Yes, it doesn't seem like the two of us have anything in common, but it just goes to show, don't prejudge people, keep an open mind, and you might find out we have more in common than we have differences," said Cody.

"Turns out we became friends right here while watching rodeo," replied Daryl.

"Rodeo? It's exciting on TV," Tegan said.

"Ever been to one?" asked Daryl.

"I've been to a few live events in Texas."

"You should go to more. It's a lot more exciting in person," replied Daryl.

"I'll look into it."

"One of the biggest ones is happening in the next month or two out west. It's one of the few winter ones too. The Sheridan WYO Winter Rodeo out in Wyoming. But I heard there is a new one starting soon in Montana, out near Yellowstone. The winter rodeos are becoming popular out there and they added a couple of new locations to make it more of a circuit and take advantage of the developing public interest."

"Doubt I can make it. I need to figure out what this mysterious creature in Owensville is and how to contain it so that it isn't causing tension in town."

"We can help some with that," said Cody.

"I'm listening," replied Tegan.

"I saw that animal out riding with Matt. Almost ran it over," replied Daryl. "And… Like I mentioned last night, I've seen it before that. Coming out here to watch rodeo with Cody," replied Daryl.

"What did you see?" she asked.

"A big cat. The biggest cat I've ever seen," began Cody.

"Yes, it was just here in the parking lot back in the corner by the woods there," said Daryl. "We were leaving the bar about the same time after watching the rodeo events. I saw something scoot across the back edge out there. I first thought it was panther or something before I realized that wouldn't make sense here in Indiana."

"But bigger," added Cody.

"Was it black?" asked Tegan.

"Couldn't tell. It was dusk, so everything looked black. That was just the first animal that popped into my head when I saw a big cat. Might have been black or might have been like a mountain lion or something like that," said Daryl. "But one other thing stood out. As it ran, I saw it had six legs."

"It only took a few seconds for it to cover the width of that parking lot and disappear into those woods. But it was taller and more muscular. I figured it was a lion, but that was even more unlikely. That's the largest and most muscular of the large cats I've seen," replied Cody. "Although I have never seen an animal with six legs."

"It's a lot of farmland between where I live off 775 and this bar. Not much in between, so he could travel and be unseen," said Daryl.

"I don't know of any lions or panthers in Indiana. The most muscular cat in this country is the jaguar. I've seen reports of southern Arizona and New Mexico, but nothing in this area, and those don't have six legs," said Tegan.

"Some of those lions can get hefty," replied Cody. "I read that the heaviest wild lion ever recorded weighed over seven hundred pounds. He killed a man in South Africa in the mid-1930s and they put him down."

"I don't think he's here either, but I will check out the parking lot on my way to see if I can find any footprints," Tegan said. "Maybe something escaped from a zoo or circus?"

"I wouldn't think he's here either, but there was a similar instance to what we've got going on now back in 1935, so that's the same timeline," Cody replied.

"A guy at the Iron Horse mentioned something about that," Tegan said.

"That's the talk around the town," said Daryl. "People talk about old man Hunt all the time. Something they don't talk about so much is the one before that," said Daryl.

"One before that?" asked Tegan.

"You stayin' for a drink?" asked Daryl.

"You've got me hooked. I'll have a beer," she said.

Cody motioned for the server, and a young lady came from the back kitchen.

"Hey, I'm Isadora. Are you ready to order?"

Tegan looked up at the guys.

"Yes, I'm ready if you are."

"Ladies first," replied Daryl.

"Dark Souls," Tegan ordered.

"Belgian Quad. Not too shabby," replied Cody. "I like their stuff. Sign of the Dragon," he said to Isadora.

"Bo & Luke," replied Daryl.

"I've heard a lot about that one," added Tegan. "I have a couple of friends back in Austin who are big stout fans."

Isadora turned and headed behind the bar while Tegan turned her attention to the two guys. "About the sighting before 1935?" Tegan again asked.

"That one goes back to 1908. Out at Miss Clara's place," added Daryl. Tegan noted he looked around the bar before he spoke.

"Miss Clara?" asked Tegan, as she also looked around the bar as she asked, but was unsure why.

"Yes, the stories in the papers right now are from Miss Ellie Orr. She's the widow who lives out on the farm near the coal mine. That land she lives on has been in the family for lifetimes. Back in 1908, her grandma lived there and encountered a similar creature. It killed hogs and disappeared into the woods when chased by some locals. No one ever mentioned the creature until the sightings picked up in 1935," added Daryl.

Isadora returned with the drinks. Tegan picked up the quad and took a sip.

"And now again. At the same property," said Tegan.

"Seems like that's one place you want to check out," replied Cody.

"Yes, Matt mentioned Ellie's name. I didn't know about her grandma," she said. "Seems like a few grandmas have had some secrets."

"If you go out there, you'll want to get her neighbor Jacob over too," added Cody. "He looks after the place."

"It's her land, but he operates the hog farm," replied Daryl. "Just like it was back in the day."

"When it was Clara's place?" asked Tegan.

"Yes, when she lived there, her neighbors, the Saygers, lived next door, and the old man looked after her," replied Daryl.

"I'll head out there this afternoon and see if I can get someone. I've been trying to track down Jerry. Seems to be a friend of yours, Daryl?"

"Yes, we are in the same club with Ronnie and Matt," he said as he panned the room again.

"Everything okay? You look around and seem nervous. Last night you said you wanted to meet in person and were nervous to give much information. I wouldn't think a big guy like you would be nervous about anything."

"The government. You know… it's always listening," said Daryl.

"Why would they be listening to us?" Tegan asked.

"Forgive my friend," replied Cody. "He has come around to craft beer, but he's still one of those conspiracy guys. Thinks Bigfoot is real," laughed Cody.

"I heard that… but who's to say he's not?" she said. "Stranger things have happened."

"They are real, and the government is in on it," Daryl said.

"I don't know about that," replied Tegan.

"Oh they are. All those mysterious creatures in the news. You know there's more of them found every day.

"Well, yeah. There are a lot of mysterious things…" she said, trailing off.

"Where do you think they are all coming from? The government's behind it. That's why there's an increase in the number of sightings," Daryl said.

"Don't you think it's because there are more people out there, cool people maybe, who search for these animals and take them more seriously?" inquired Tegan.

"I get it. That's what you're doing now, but I tell ya. Keep sticking your nose in things like this, and you're bound to draw their attention," Daryl said.

"Still, I'll take my chances," said Cody. "No need hiding in shadows and speaking in code on the phone."

"I'm just saying," said Daryl.

"You're not doing anything wrong, so I shouldn't worry about it," Tegan said.

She finished her drink and stood up. "It was nice meeting you guys, and I appreciate the updates. I need to find Jerry, then head out to Ellie's place," Tegan said.

She reached out to shake their hands and thank them for the information. The men stood to return the gesture. As she turned to leave, a man at the bar raised his head and watched her exit from the reflection in the mirror behind the bar. He wore sunglasses, a black StarShield logo hat, and a navy-blue StarShield t-shirt with the agency's emblem. He watched in silence as she left before he lowered his head and took a sip from the straw in his barnyard soda.

Tegan left the bar and drove down State Route 64 until she turned left on State Route 65. A right turn onto County Road 250 became County Road 275 before it changed into County Road 775. A sharp right turned beside a bank of mailboxes and brought her to a gravel driveway that continued to a fork in the road. She took the branch off to the left and the gravel road led to a group of buildings across from a small pond. One building was Jerry Morgan's house.

"Hello, Jerry. I'm Tegan. I spoke to a friend of yours and I was hoping to get a moment of your time," she said to the man as he stood outside the front door.

"How 'ya doin'? Nice to see ya," said the portly biker. Like Ronnie, he was a middle-aged man with a long, gray ponytail. He wore a Harley t-shirt and denim jeans, and although he was not wearing the biker club jacket, she was certain he had one inside. She walked closer to shake his hand and noticed a small tool shed, a large barn, and a covered building where he stored his motorcycles.

"Ronnie said you saw a big six-legged cat the other day. Seems like it could hide well around this place," Tegan said.

"There are plenty of trees, some hills, the pond. I bet it could do well around here. But we saw it riding into town," he clarified.

"Do you know Ellie Orr? I heard she lives around here."

"Yes, Miss Ellie lives just up the road off 675," he said.

"I heard she spotted the creature on her property and the papers picked up on it," replied Tegan.

"Yeah, I heard about that. I haven't seen her to ask about it, but I am sure it's the same creature," he commented.

"What did you see?"

"The road was tree-lined on both sides, and it ran right out in front of us. Just missed it," replied Jerry.

"Did you get a good look at it? All I have heard about it is that it is a large cat with six legs."

"Big and muscular. It got across the road real quick and was gone. I just got a blur because I wasn't expecting to see something. Especially something that big to shoot out of there. I saw its eyes were bright yellow, like little glowing suns, and it seemed to be a light brown color like a lion or cougar," he added. "The six legs threw me off. I sort of dismissed it as just my imagination on account of how quickly it moved."

"How far is it from your property out to the church where you saw it?" she asked.

"Not but maybe four miles. It's doable if you're thinking about Miss Ellie's," Jerry added.

"Yes, that would be an easy distance for a cat like that," Tegan stated. "I just talked to your friend Daryl earlier today. He and another friend spotted it," she said.

"Seems to make its way around town. Granted, the town ain't very big," said Jerry.

"Seems that way. I'm trying to identify what it is, why it's here, and how to get it out of the area. I want to get some eyes on it and get it out of here so the town folk can sleep at night," replied Tegan.

"Us boys in the bike club and most of the farmers in this area know how to handle a rifle. We can take care of it, and I know a few who tried," Jerry said.

"Next, I'm going over to Ellie's and see what I can learn from her. Maybe it's still in this area and we can capture it."

"Good luck. Call me if you need some help if you decide to go huntin' for it," offered Jerry.

"I'll keep that in mind. If I do search for it, I will need some help. I have experience investigating things like this, but with a team. This time I'm alone. Thanks for your help. I'll be in touch," Tegan said.

Tegan turned right out of Jerry's place and went back the way she drove until County Road 250. This time she turned right on County Road 675 South. To the left, she saw a large brick ranch-style house surrounded by fields of corn. Next to it, an old farmhouse backed up against the hills. As she opened the door of her car, the smell hit her and alerted her to the fact she had arrived at a hog farm.

She walked to the front porch, knocked on the door, and waited for a response. Soon, an elderly woman appeared at the door.

"Yes?" she asked in a shaky voice.

"Hello, Miss Ellie? My name is Tegan, and I wanted to ask you a few questions about the animal you saw the other day? It was in the newspaper?"

"Oh yes, come in. My neighbor Jacob works the farm here. He's here visiting if you want to come in. I just put on a kettle of tea.

"That would be lovely," she said as she took the opened door and headed inside toward the dimly lit kitchen.

"Nice to meet you," she said as she approached Jacob. "This is a nice place you have here," Tegan said.

"Thank you. It's been in my family for over a hundred years now," Ellie replied. "Can you believe it?"

"I heard your family has seen this animal over the years as well," stated Tegan.

"That's a fact. My grandmother was one of the first to see it. Right here on this property. She didn't know what it was and contacted her neighbor to come over. Jacob is Jacob Saygers III. His grandfather, Jacob Saygers, lived next door and had a hired hand who helped him around the farm. They went out looking for the creature," Ellie remembered.

"Your grandmother's name was Clara?"

"Yes. Jacob's grandfather was sixty-two when he saw an animal in the hogs," said Ellie.

"Sixty-two? And he was hunting mysterious creatures? I hope I can still do it at that age," Tegan said.

"He lived a long time. He was a retired farmer and lived here until he was eighty-one. Moved out to Phoenix and lived his final three years out there," Ellie said.

"It's great he was there to look after your mom," Tegan said.

"Yes, he was good to mom after dad died," she answered.

"What happened to your dad?" asked Tegan.

"He died when I was young. He was just forty-two, speaking of young," Ellie said.

"That is young. Do you mind if I asked what happened to him?" Tegan replied.

"My dad, William, died on a trip out of town," Ellie said, as she took a seat and sipped her tea. "He went almost two hours away up in Columbus. He bought some hogs from the Bartholomew County Fair. We had one of the first cars in the city, a 1905 Jewell Stanhope. It was brand new, and he wanted to drive up and show it off at the fair," she said.

"A car in 1905? That must have been special," Tegan said.

"He was a great farmer around here and made a lot of money. He bought the pigs and signed the papers at the bank to ship them down here by rail. The hogs made it, but daddy didn't," she added.

"Did they say what happened to him?" asked Tegan.

"They ruled it as some mischievous teenagers out by the water inside Mill Race Park. Police said they saw the car and thought he had some money on him, but…," Ellie faded off

"But?" asked Tegan.

"But she doesn't believe that story," added Jacob.

"What do you think happened?" asked Tegan.

"I don't know. But years later, when she and I were young, they said there was some kind of creature discovered out there in the seventies," Steve said.

"Our family seems to be plagued by unknown creatures. First Daddy, then grandma's farm, and now this," Ellie realized.

"I'm here to identify this creature and remove him from this land," Tegan said.

"That's good. You're just in time because we lost another hog last night, so he's still around," replied Ellie.

"I plan to find out what's in with your hogs," returned Tegan.

"I know what it is," Ellie said.

"What is it?

"I'm afraid history seems to repeat itself. I think the Wampus Beast is back!" Ellie concluded.

"Wampus Beast?" replied Tegan. "What is the Wampus Beast?"

"It's a creature heard whining about camps at night. They say it is a spiritual, yellow-eyed cat, having occult powers, and smelled like a mixture of skunk and wet dog. It has six legs and uses them to climb mountains and dash across the ground."

"That sounds like an incredible description. Something I haven't encountered before. I have heard others report about its cries and the six legs. I haven't heard of the name Wampus beast before," replied Tegan.

"That's what Jacob's grandfather called what he chased out of here back then," replied Ellie.

"I'm going to need a team to investigate this creature," replied Tegan.

"Count me in," said Jacob. "If my granddaddy went after this animal, and it's back, I'm taking it up this time!"

11 Miss Ellie's Farm

Mid-morning the next day, Tegan returned to Ellie Mae Orr's farm. Jacob Saygers III was already at the house with Ellie in anticipation of Tegan's arrival. He had a fleece lined tan hunting jacket and a rifle ready to search the fields and hills that surrounded the farm for clues. Moments later, an old, red pickup truck pulled into the driveway. It was Daryl Hartmann, ready to join the excursion.

"Mornin' boys," Tegan said as her newly assembled team arrived on site. "I made a call yesterday to Ivy Tech Community College up in Princeton and could pick up a thermal camera for our investigation."

"I didn't know if you had any protection, so I brought a couple of revolvers for you," said Daryl, as he handed over two Ruger Super Blackhawks with .454 Casull ammunition. He mounted one weapon with a scope base and one-inch rings with a Bushnell Elite 2x-6x-32mm 3500 handgun scope.

"I came out the other night when Ellie called. Me and a friend set out to find the animal when she heard the hogs acting up in the pens," said Jacob.

"Losing those hogs must be difficult for you. I bet you came running quick. Did you see anything unusual?" asked Tegan.

"Yeah, I noticed something unusual. I got a decent video of it on my phone if you want to have a look at what we're going up against."

"Hell yeah, I wanna see it," Tegan said.

"Get ready for this," he said as he pulled up the video and Tegan, Daryl, and Miss Ellie leaned in to get a closer look.

"I got her call and drove up to the north pasture on my side-by-side to see if I could locate any missing pigs. I got up there and seen something out of the corner of my eye – something big. Just kind of slinking off down the hill. I quickly took out my phone and turned on the video camera. I was lucky to get something, but it was just the tail end of what I saw up there," Jacob said.

"Hit play on that bad boy!" added Daryl.

The video showed the hillside near dusk. The medium gray of impending nightfall draped the trees and landscape, when the silhouette of a large, obvious cat casually walked along the top ridge of the hill and down the side.

"I'll be damned!" said Daryl.

"Look at the size of that thing!" added Tegan.

"It's ridiculous. I can't keep losing my hogs. And I'm afraid if it comes around the house, something might happen to Miss Ellie. She is older and can't take care of herself against a creature like this," explained Jacob.

"No, it would be on her before she knew she was even in danger," stated Tegan. "I'd be interested to see where you shot this video."

"I can take you there," Jacob said.

The two men and Tegan got into the vehicle and drove toward the barn. The smaller hogs scattered. They drove past the pens and through the pasture, while Tegan reviewed the farm.

"You've got some good-looking hogs out here. What's their approximate average weight?"

"Up in the pens we've got mostly weaners that are two or three-months-olds and are no longer reliant on their mother's milk. Those we raise to about six months, and they go maybe two-fifty. The ones out to pasture range from three hundred to over seven hundred. Maybe a little bigger. They breed domestics to be heavier and some of these larger ones might hit nine hundred to a thousand," Jacob replied.

"Nine hundred? Is that so? That's a big hog," replied Tegan.

"They can get up there. The biggest hog on record is ole Big Bill. He stood about five feet high and over twenty-five hundred pounds," added Jacob.

"That's some bacon right there!" shouted Daryl.

"He was a Poland China, and those are big fellers. They are big-framed, long, muscular, and lean. One of the oldest breeds and biggest. The Shaker Society of Union Village raised them in Warren County, Ohio. That's out around Lebanon, close to Cincinnati. I know you said you were from Texas. You ever been out to Cincinnati?" asked Jacob.

For a second, there was a chink in the newly hardened exterior of Tegan as she thought of the events over the last few months. Her head dropped as the memories returned, but just as quickly as the feeling came, it vanished, and she picked her head back up and held it high.

"Once."

"These guys out here are pretty heavy right now, being cold weather. It would take something mighty big to drag one off," replied Daryl.

"Looking at that video, I thought that animal looked like it was five-hundred pounds or better, so he could do that easily," replied Tegan.

"I can only imagine what that would do to a person. Especially someone like Miss Ellie!" Daryl responded.

"It's a nice farm here, surrounded by a dense wooded area, and deep valleys between the hills. An ideal place for it to be living because he has plenty of cover to hide in these hills and a ready meal supply down here with the hogs," said Tegan. "Any other neighbors report any missing livestock? When my friends and I investigated the chupacabra in San Antonio, it was a small farming community like this one, and a few local ranchers suffered losses of cattle. That's their livelihood."

"That's the same with me. This is all I've got. The farm has been in Ellie's family for generations, but my family has been farming it for almost as long. I've been farming here my whole life," replied Jacob. "She lets me use the land for hogs, and I pay her a fee for its usage. I get some land for my hogs and she gets some money out of the deal. Losing more hogs would affect us both."

The side-by-side slowed as they approached the back of the pasture.

"This is where it was?" asked Tegan.

"It was coming down this way. I saw something out of the corner of my eye and tried to get the phone out real quick. Next thing I knew there it was on that little hill, and it walked off to the right, then it was gone. It was dusk. I saw the silhouette, but I got little detail on it. I could tell it looked like it had short, matted fur," Jacob stated.

"Let's get up on that hill and look for tracks. Maybe we can find a trail to see where it's been traveling," said Tegan. "Since this is where you saw it just a couple of days ago, this is where we should start our investigation. Maybe he's still here. Being daytime, he might be bedded down up here. There's an excellent source of food here, so I expect he's likely to stay around a while."

The trio exited the side-by-side and looked up to scan the hillside for any movement. The wind increased, which created some sound from the branches of the empty trees.

"That snow we had the other day hasn't melted yet. That will help us locate any footprints," said Daryl as he pointed toward the ground. "You can see some prints left by the hogs here. This is a high traffic area. The weight of the hogs has mashed down the snow and mixed it up with mud. Some of these tracks are indistinguishable now. These hogs are in sight for an animal lurking up on that ridge. But up on that hill there shouldn't be much traffic, so the tracks we're looking for should still be there."

Starting up the hill, the snow was about four to five inches deep. Enough to provide coverage to track the animal. The air was chilly, and the skies were overcast, but at least no snow was falling. Less than ten minutes in, they stopped as Daryl pointed out a fresh track.

"Look here. These tracks are recent. You can see how the snow has filled up the track. That means it's newer than yesterday morning when we got that bit of new snow. It looks like it's headin' up the hill, a return trip from its visit to the farm," Daryl reported.

"Let's get on this thing and track it," Jacob said.

"We'll see how it goes. Let's see if we can find this cat," replied Tegan as they started toward the first track. The snow crunched under their feet as they made their way higher up the hill. Small twigs and ground flora snapped and crunched with each step on their ascension.

"Right here. Our first scrape from this cat," announced Daryl, who pointed to a spot in the snow that showed the animal had been in the area. "That's him marking his territory. It's a signal of social interaction to show territory, dominance, and a breeding calling card."

"Breeding? I hope there are no more of them in the area," said Tegan.

"Chances are there would have to be another large cat, like a tiger or lion, and I can assure you there's none of them in the area," said Jacob. "I've covered these hills since I was knee-high to a June bug."

"This one had to come from somewhere. They have sighted it multiple times over more than a hundred years, so it can't be the same individual animal," suggested Tegan.

"First scrape is a good sign he's here. Let's keep on him and see where he goes," said Daryl.

"Here's another scrape. Looks like we're on the right track," pointed out Jacob. "He's marking his territory for something. We better lock and load just in case we come up on him quicker than expected."

"Here's another track," spotted Daryl. "He's headed down this side of the hill. There's a creek down there. That's where he's headed."

They continued along a lightly worn trail that headed down the backside of the hill toward the creek below. They still followed the tracks as the fallen snow betrayed the cat. The ground coverage was patchier in spots as they neared the base of the hill and approached the creek. Despite the cold temperatures, the small creek ran rapidly and gave an audible identification. The fresh flowing stream would provide a welcomed source of water for the cat and other wildlife in the area.

Near the creek, the trail became more difficult to walk as debris and fallen logs cluttered the base of the hill. The group of trackers moved slowly, careful of their footing as the snow became wetter and slicker as it mixed with the moisture of the brook.

The team stayed close to the trail until they found an area that had very little snow, which made it more difficult to spot any tracks. The three hunters fanned out, to look for more snow that would allow them to continue their pursuit. Jacob noticed deeper snow above the sparsely covered area, but he didn't see any tracks, which suggested the animal did not go that way. Tegan crossed over the creek and searched another area with heavier snow covering.

"Hey guys, I've got tracks!" she yelled. The two male companions stopped and moved down to join her on the other side of the creek.

"Looks like he went down here to the creek bottom and then up this other side," said Daryl. He removed a pair of binoculars from his pouch and scanned the area above. "Got him. The tracks continue all the way up the side of this other hill."

The snow on the side of the other hill was deeper as the prior hill shielded it from the wind.

"Here's the trail. Several tracks in the area show our animal's path," said Jacob.

"Look at the size of these tracks and how closely spaced they are," said Daryl. "Bigger cats like bobcats and lions move slowly and stealthily, often looking for prey. These tracks are close together as well, which shows this cat wasn't in a hurry. He didn't chase something wild that he'd have to capture. He knows where the food is and that it can't get away."

"Remember the sightings of this creature have suggested it has six legs. That could also account for the close spacing," added Tegan.

The number of trees increased as the team climbed further up the hill. It reduced the amount of snow on the ground and made it more difficult to track the animal. The availability of solid tracks decreased, but the trio could still locate an occasional track. That proved they were still on the animal's trail.

More than an hour into the hunt, the weather took a turn for the worse as snow fell again and increased the risk that the tracks would soon start to fill and become more difficult to find.

"We need to pick up the pace and track him as fast as we can before we lose its track," suggested Tegan.

"I don't know. This weather is picking up. I hope we can find him," said Daryl.

"Let's keep going. This snow is coming down, and it's already covering up the ground pretty good," observed Jacob.

They continued for a while but didn't locate additional tracks. Then, as their hope diminished somewhat, excitement once again grew when they found what appeared to be a fresh bed. From that point on, the tracks were fresh and appeared to zig zag throughout the area. It was a sign that the animal was aware it was being tracked. However, time soon ran out as the snow continued to increase in speed and density. It covered the tracks along the trail and made it impossible to continue to track the cat.

"I think we should call it. We've been out here a few hours and covered a couple of miles. It's a little disappointing because it seemed like we were closing in, but now this snow is making it too difficult to see where we're going," reported Tegan. "Let's get back to the house and warm up. I'd like to make a few calls and get another investigation set up. I also want to learn more about this Wampus Beast, as Miss Ellie called it."

"Sounds about right. It's going to get dark in a bit, and if we are close to it, we might be in a bad spot once the sun goes down," replied Daryl. "It has much better night vision that we do."

It was another hour before the group returned to Ellie's house, and as she frequently did, she had a pot of tea at the ready for her guests. She welcomed them back and readied each a cup as they sat around the wooden kitchen table and discussed their pursuit of the elusive beast.

"I know we didn't get eyes on him today, but I think we were close," said Tegan.

"Once that snow kicked up and started coming down as hard and fast as it did, that put an end to it," recalled Daryl. "We could have spent hours after that just walking around in circles, not knowing where we were or where the cat was. That could have put all of us in danger real quick."

"Here's some blackberry sage tea. That'll warm you up," Ellie said to each of the hunters. "You'll get that cat. I know it."

Back in Tegan's apartment, she reflected on the day with some soccer and a bag of movie theater popcorn. She opened her laptop and searched for the Wampus Beast to seek more information on what she was up against. She found mention of a Wampus Beast attributed to the death of livestock that ranged from North Carolina to Georgia in the 1920s to 1930s. That fit within the timeframe of her accused creature. Other similar sightings included a creature in Missouri called the Gallywampus, the Whistling Wampus in Arkansas, and the Wampus Cat in the Appalachian region. They knew it throughout the Midwest, and that included Indiana and parts of Ohio. She didn't want any internet mumbo jumbo. She needed to know what was out there in the woods and threatened the Town of

Owensville.

She sought an expert and located a number for a local facility for exotic felines. She wasn't sure what she was up against, but *exotic feline* fit the bill for this creature. It was an exotic animal, and she knew it was rare. Already closed for the evening, she left a message and hoped for a return call in the morning.

12 Limitlessly Liminal

Tegan's cell phone rang just after 9:30 a.m., which caused her to awkwardly slow jog from the kitchen to the living room to pick it up in time.

"Hello?"

"Hi… is this Tegan? My name is Dr. Thomas Normandy, one director at the Exotic Feline Rescue Center in Center Point," the man said. "You left us a message about an exotic cat?"

"Hi, yes, Dr. Normandy. I'm surprised you called so early. I didn't think you opened until later."

"Yes, we don't. I'm not working in the Center today, but I retrieved the overnight voicemails and yours particularly caught my attention. You said you think you saw something?"

"I haven't seen it myself, but several locals have. Down in Owensville," Tegan replied.

"Oh yes, that. I saw a couple of stories in the newspaper about an enormous cat in the area, but I had not seen anyone get a close look at it, capture it, or heard it attacked anyone. We have not investigated. I dismiss most of the these as misidentifications," Dr. Normandy replied.

"What do you know about the Wampus Beast?" asked Tegan.

"The what?"

"Wampus Beast. Some call it Wampus Cat," clarified Tegan.

"We help real exotic felines that are injured or need to be rescued. Ones that cannot live out in the wild on their own. That sort of thing. We don't research mythology," he replied.

"Whatever is out there is real. I saw a video of the animal and I went out tracking it last night," she said.

"And what did you find?" asked Dr. Normandy.

"We found a recent bed and we found large tracks in the immediate area. Giant tracks. Bigger than any I've ever seen before," she said.

"And you've seen… a large variety of tracks before?"

"I've seen my share," she added.

"Sid you actually see this… Wampus Beast?" Dr. Normandy questioned.

"No, not yet, but…"

"Until I, or somebody else, sees this animal in the flesh, I will not believe an urban legend lives among us," he stated.

"There's more than one that lives amongst us," answered Tegan.

"What makes you think this creature is a mythical animal?" he asked.

"One witness saw the damage it did to hogs on her land. In 1935 another local farmer spotted a similar creature on his land, and even older than that, my witness' grandmother saw the same animal on the same farm more than a hundred years ago," Tegan provided. "That's why I am trying to get information on what this animal is."

"I still don't know that the animal you are trying to track is the same thing as the Wampus Beast," he replied. "But I can give you information on the Wampus Beast."

"That's all I'm looking for," answered Tegan.

"I'm afraid it is just legend - popular folklore stories in the Deep South and Appalachian regions. There is a brewery in Virginia called Strangeways Brewing and it brews a triple IPA called Wampus Cat, which is named after the legend," added Dr. Normandy.

"A brewery? That's right up my alley," replied Tegan.

"If you want to talk more about it, perhaps we could meet in person. I don't want to discuss more over the phone," Dr. Normandy said.

"I'm not sure why people are reluctant to discuss this animal over the phone, but I want to learn more about it. Where and when is a good time for you?"

"You said a brewery was your thing. Since I'm not going in today. We could meet somewhere for lunch. The Feline Center is about two hours away from you, which I know is a far drive. I live up in Bloomfield, a little closer, but still far. How about we meet somewhere in between? There is an excellent spot in Vincennes to grab lunch and a drink?"

"Sounds good to me," she replied.

"I don't want to be on the phone or too close to the Center speaking about something crazy like the Wampus Cat," Dr. Normandy replied.

Just after twelve Tegan arrived at Vincennes Brewing. It was in an historic brick building. Inside, exposed brick walls were covered with historical photos. They mounted a large black menu board on a wall near the bar. The brewery offered a quartz covered bar top and multiple wooden tables in an open room. Having only opened at eleven, the number of customers was small, which made it easy for Tegan to locate Dr. Normandy, who already awaited her at a table near the bar.

"You must be Dr. Normandy," Tegan said as she approached the table.

"Tegan? Yes, call me Tom. Thanks for meeting me. Talking on the phone about unknown creatures is a little awkward. Plus, we receive a lot of prank calls. Meeting in person is a way to ensure there is at least a credible report," he said.

"I understand. I have investigated claims of mysterious creatures as well, and sometimes the reports are bogus. But, I assure you this is legitimate," Tegan said. "I saw the reports in the paper about an unknown animal in the town. One of my witnesses stated it was the Wampus, and not just that, but she said, *It's back*," added Tegan. "I wasn't familiar with the Wampus Cat."

"Did you want to order something first?" asked Tom. "They don't have the Strangeways Wampus Cat, but they have a triple IPA called Fat Cat. That's what I'll have," he said.

Tegan observed the menu and noted it contained a Passionfruit Berliner Weisse, but she passed it up for a RendezBrew pilsner. She found that after the events in Cincinnati, her tastes in many things, especially beer, had changed. Now she preferred pilsners, especially foeder-aged pilsners and lagers.

"Now that we have that settled, about your cat. They say the Wampus Cat originated in Cherokee folklore. Some say it is a half-dog, half-cat creature that can run erect or on all fours," Tom said. "The Wampus cat varies in appearance, but is feline. It is depicted as a cougar or mountain lion, but often with black fur and yellow eyes. When it attacks, it lets out a strange, high-pitched hissing sound. Some sightings say it has four legs like a normal cat, but others report the animal has six legs. Four for running and two for fighting. The six-legged creature is rarer. There is a statue depicting it on the campus of a junior high school in Conway, Arkansas."

"I didn't mention this when we first talked, but from what I saw in the video, this cat had six legs, so it's interesting that you mentioned that first. The tracks we found were close together," replied Tegan.

"In our call I mentioned Strangeways Brewing. The brewery describes the creature as a half-woman, half-mountain lion that walks on hind legs and has four additional sharp-clawed appendages. It also picks up on another description from the legend – the ability to drive people crazy. The creature is said to have glowing, hypnotic eyes."

"Most of the witnesses have described yellow glowing eyes, but I haven't heard of a person coming close enough to become mentally affected by the creature. At least not hypnotically," replied Tegan. "You mentioned the tracks. Some legends describe the tracks as eighteen to twenty inches apart while walking, but when running it covers the ground in tremendous leaps of from six to ten feet."

"I can see that. What we saw were close together. We haven't seen tracks from it running, but I have witnesses who saw it run and described it as quick," added Tegan. "They said in size, it was larger than any cat they have ever seen. And these are farmers and hunters who have spent their lives in the woods and the fields in the area. They have seen many animals. This one has them shook," Tegan added.

"Non-Native cultures say it has luminous yellow eyes that can pierce through people's souls and drive them insane. One thing people agree on is that the Wampus Cat roams around just after dark to look for its prey," said Tom.

"That's exactly when he is hunting. The farm in question lost a couple of hogs over the past few weeks, and when I visited this week, the farm's owner mentioned they just lost another the night before. This cat stays up in the hills beyond the pasture and comes down at night whenever it's hungry. It has plenty of cover to stay hidden, moves at night when no one sees it, and it has a large buffet of pork just waiting for it," she said.

"Stories about loss of livestock are common in modern sightings. People around Mooresville, North Carolina blame the Wampus Cat for killing livestock. I've read about it down in Alabama. The McDowell News wrote about how some people in Alabama claimed the government tried to create a Wampus Cat-like creature that escaped a facility and now roams the lands," said Tom. "But I don't believe those wild government conspiracy theories."

"It seems far-fetched… although, I know the government has had its eye on cryptids for many years. I found a cache of files in an underground lab out in Arizona. The cabinets were filled with reports, newspaper articles, and top-secret information about many unknown creatures around the country, and even the world," revealed Tegan. "I think they were just tracking them, for national security reasons. I don't know why they would create one. Just rumors is my guess."

"What's your next step with this cat?" asked Tom.

"Me and two guys from the area where the cat was last seen are going out tomorrow morning to see it for ourselves," replied Tegan.

"And what if you do?"

"Then, we'll see. I promised Ms. Orr we would get it out of the area and off her property. I would hate to kill it, but this is the third story I have heard about this same or a similar animal in that area spanning a timeframe of more than one hundred years," stated Tegan.

"There are no exotic cats that have a lifespan that long, and I can say that with certainty," replied Tom.

"Agreed, but the question is, whatever it is, why does it keep coming back?" asked Tegan. "And for that, I think we need to get out there and take this one down."

"Whatever it is, you know it is a wild animal, and any wild animal will put up a fight if you corner it," said Tom. "How are you planning on fighting it?"

"The guys I tracked with yesterday had rifles just in case we ran up on it, and I had two revolvers. But any unknown animal, I don't want to kill it unless necessary. If it is an out of place known wild animal, it needs to be captured and moved. If it is a new species, it needs to be studied. It hasn't killed people yet but based on its size and the proximity to my witnesses' house, and her age, I am afraid something could happen, even if it's accidental," Tegan stated.

Tegan's phone dinged with an alert of a new message. She removed the phone from her jeans' pocket and saw a message from what she recognized as Jacob's number.

Got another video last night. Check this out!

The message was accompanied by a video attachment that played when she clicked it. She watched it for a moment before a large black cat came into sight. She watched as the creature prowled through the pen near Ellie's house, searched for a smaller pig, one of the weaners that Jacob mentioned in her initial visit, and attacked it. With its fast reflexes, massive paws, and large teeth, the hog did not stand a chance. She shook her head, laid the phone on the table, and pushed it toward Tom.

"Maybe this will change your mind," she said.

Tom drew the phone closer and pushed play on the video. He watched in silence as the video replayed showing better visual evidence of an unknown six-legged creature that appeared to mirror the urban legends of the Wampus Beast more than he had ever seen. Afterward he looked up and quietly stared at Tegan for a moment. He slid the phone back toward her and asked, "This farm. What's the address and what time are you going to be there tomorrow?"

13 Caution: Danger

The group of Tegan, Jacob, Daryl, and Dr. Normandy met at Miss Ellie's farmhouse late in the evening, close to 9 p.m. As usual, Miss Ellie had a pot of tea on for her guests. This time she also had some light snacks just in case they got hungry out on the hill during the night.

They tracked at night with the hope they could catch the animal during its active times. The snow came down, much heavier than it had been all week. Despite the conditions, Tegan felt confident and not scared, as she had been in the past on nighttime investigations.

Miss Ellie poured a round of Guayusa tea for each of her guests and one for herself. Jacob interrupted the enjoyment of the tea.

"Hey everyone, before we get started, I just wanted to thank Tegan for coming out here and attempting to put this creature and its attacks behind us. It has been nice meeting and working with you over the past several days, and with Dr. Normandy's background in exotic cats. I think we have a good chance of getting this bastard tonight," he said. "As a thank you, I bought a bottle of wine. I thought we would have a small, good luck drink before we head out tonight."

He sat the bottle on the table and went to get a few glasses. Tegan picked up the bottle and after she read the label, she clarified the gift.

"What kind of wine is this, Jacob?"

"I don't know. I don't drink wine, but I saw it in the store, and it stood out to me. It's a white wine. That's all I know," he said.

"It's not a wine. It's kind of like wine. It's a mead from Oliver Winery. Some people call mead a honey wine. Maybe that's why you thought it was a wine? But it's Camelot, an orange-blossom honey mead. Should be good. Light and sweet," she said.

"I don't know. I'm a Miller Lite guy myself, but I figured you liked wine or some other fancy drink," Jacob replied.

"This might be out of your comfort zone, but it's good. Just remember, it will be sweet," she said as she emptied the bottle amongst the group of glasses.

"You want one, Miss Ellie?" she asked

Miss Ellie looked surprised and playfully gasped. "Oh my, child. None for me. I haven't had a drink in years," she said with a giggle.

"Suit yourself," replied Tegan as she poured the bottle between the four hunters.

"I don't figure this will warm us up like a whiskey would," added Daryl, "But if it brings us luck with that animal, down the hatch it goes."

"Cheers to a good hunt," announced Jacob as he hoisted his drink in the air. The others soon joined in the celebration.

"Here! Here!" they all said, then downed the contents in unison.

Once the glasses touched the table, the group turned with Daryl as he led the way and held open the door for the others. As soon as they stepped outside, the wind smacked them in the face.

"We ready for this? asked Jacob.

"Ready!" shouted the remaining party.

They walked from the house, down the gravel driveway, and to the hog pen. Jacob opened the gate to allow everyone entry. The ground was muddy, but still covered with snow from the past couple of days. The snow within the pen was patchy and scattered with mud and hog footprints. Some prints were worn from where other pigs had laid and wallowed.

The pigs didn't care to notice the men and woman who walked amongst them. They viewed the invaders as a non-threat and detected they did not bring food or anything of interest for the hogs. Near the front of the pasture, just past the smaller pen for weaners, small sheds used by the hogs for shelter appeared.

With the moon brighter and the wind not as strong as it was the other night, the trek through the front end of the pasture was quiet, except for the frequent grunts of multiple hogs as the group passed.

The team searched the ground, but there was no sign of the predator.

Its most recent trip was now obscured by over four inches of snow and turned up mud from the travel of the large number of hogs in the pasture over the past two-day period.

"It's been a few days that we know of since the animal was last here in the pasture," stated Tegan. "Keep your eyes open for deeper snow in the less traveled areas. Maybe we can pick up a set of tracks."

"Roger that," yelled Daryl.

Reaching the back of the pasture, the group came upon the fence, which, at five feet tall, was an obstacle for more than just Tegan. Daryl placed one booted foot on the taut galvanized **barbed wire fence** to test its sturdiness. After he verified the fence could withstand his weight, he placed a gloved hand on the top line, and swung a leg over to the other side before he jumped to the ground on the opposite side. Jacob followed next. Dr. Normandy paused and looked at the ground to the right of where the men crossed. He shot the light from his flashlight toward the ground.

"Right here. Look at the size of those prints! It is a little elongated because of the weight of the animal and the distance needed to stop, but it's shorter than I would expect. It looks like the cat wasn't strained in leaping the fence. It tells me it is graceful and controlled jump with the full weight of the animal coming down on these front tracks. Look how deep they are!" replied Tom.

"Do you believe me now?" asked Tegan.

After she asked her question, she paused and shook her head. She rose her right hand to her head and saw an image enter her mind. The vision became clear as she recalled the mead they drank inside the house. She was still new to these visions and attempted to adjust to them, but she theorized since it just kicked in, the visions must take time to appear after she drank the mead. Either that, or they were close to the animal. Possibly both. She reached her arm to block Dr. Normandy's forward progress.

"Did you bring any other weapons with you?" asked Tegan.

"Are you two coming or not?" Daryl called out from the other side of the fence.

Tegan turned and searched the area with her mind, hoping she would find some sign of their intended target. She scanned the hill ahead as she gingerly took her steps onto and over the fence. She never took her eyes off of the ridge. Dr. Normandy followed behind and joined the others on the opposite side.

"It's out there," said Tegan.

"How can you be sure?" asked Jacob.

"I can sense it," she said. "It's close."

Daryl and Jacob acknowledged the sign and loaded their weapons and then continued toward the base of the hill.

"Let's do this!" shouted Daryl.

"I brought a tranquilizer gun to anesthetize the cat, if possible," replied Dr. Normandy. "It was just in my head this morning as I set out to pack the car for the trip down here."

Tegan continued to search the hill above for more signs, a sharper image of the vision, or something else. To hunt a vicious large six-legged cat was dangerous enough, but to do it at night? That took the danger to a whole new level. But despite it, Tegan remained calm and confident.

Hello, she mentally projected.

Nothing.

Hello, she sought again.

My name is Tegan. Can you hear me?

Several seconds later, she received a response.

I-I can hear you, a shaky mental voice replied.

The animal roared from its location on the hill, startling the men below.

"Di-Did you hear that?" asked Daryl. "That thing must be huge. That sound was the loudest roar I've ever heard!"

So you can roar. It's okay. We won't hurt you. Do you have a name? thought Tegan.

My… my name is Dave, the animal replied telepathically.

Getting a response from the animal, Tegan could sense the animal was cautious, and scared, but she didn't get the impression that it wanted to attack the humans. She called an audible to adjust the team's play.

"Dr. Normandy, take the lead. Switch to the tranquilizer. We need to subdue this animal if possible," suggested Tegan. "How long would it take?"

"About ten to fifteen minutes, in most cases. This animal appeared to be bigger in the video, so we either up the minutes or the number of darts. We need five tranquilizer darts to bring it down."

She focused again on the voice she heard in her head

Dave, we don't want to hurt you, but you can't live in this area and eat these hogs. We need you to move to another place, and we're here to do that now.

I don't trust you, returned the thoughts of Dave

Why are you here in this area? thought Tegan.

I don't know. I think you will kill me, he thought, trembling.

We won't kill you, responded Tegan.

I still don't trust you.

I assure you. We won't kill you, thought Tegan. *But we need to get you out of here.*

Where will I go?

A sanctuary. Close to here. It will be a safe place for you. You can meet new friends and there will be plenty of food provided. You don't have to hunt hogs anymore, mentally replied Tegan.

Sanctuary? Has a pleasant sound to it. It's safe?

Yes, very safe.

Good, mentally replied Dave. *These coal miners are getting dangerous.*

We have to shoot you, but only with a tranquilizer. It will put you to sleep… and sting…. But it will allow us to move you out of the danger here and get you to the sanctuary, thought Tegan. *It will be quick. Will you allow us to move you to the Sanctuary?*

O-Okay. Do what you gotta do, thought the scared cat. *I know if I continue to stay here, people will continue to spread and likely kill me.*

I won't let that happen, Dave. Stay there. We'll come find you, replied Tegan.

"This way," Tegan said to the guys as she motioned with her arm and continued to move up the hill.

The group followed Tegan as she climbed further up the hill for another twenty minutes to reach the cat. Then she slowed down as she realized they were close.

We're here. Don't fight it. This will only take a second. You'll get a good nap and will wake up away from these people and in a safe environment.

Okay. I have no choice but to trust you.

"We're almost there," Tegan said to the team. "Let Dr. Normandy take the shot on this," she said to the team. "We want to anesthetize the animal. Not kill him."

Dr. Normandy listened to the sounds from the woods and hoped to locate the large, legendary cat. That would make a good exhibit for the Center. He hoped the increase in ticket sales would save the Center from the financial issues it had faced since the start of the pandemic.

"Just a little further up ahead," said Tegan. "There, ten o'clock, behind the large tree…. Dr. Normandy?"

Dr. Normandy stepped forward and scanned the area Tegan pointed out. He strained his eyes and located a dark shadow that lurked behind a large stump. The director took aim and fired.

pht pht pht

Three darts fired off from the tranquilizer. A groan emerged from the bush as they struck Dave in his muscular hind legs. The animal still leaned forward and plodded a couple of steps from the brush. Dr. Normandy paused and watched the enormous animal step onto the trail leading down to the pasture.

"Jesus, look at that size of him," gasped Jacob.

"Again," called out Tegan.

The doctor took aim once more.

pht pht

Two more shots fired from Dr. Normandy's gun. After the five shots, the beast stumbled and wobbled.

"Now we wait," said Dr. Normandy. "For an animal this size we need ample sedative, but too much of a dose could kill it. We don't want that. Let's give it a chance to work."

Dave continued to stand on shaky legs for a few minutes. He didn't move forward, but the wobble in his legs increased. He tried again to walk down the hill, but after a couple of slow and deliberate steps, Dave collapsed to the ground.

"Now we have to move in!" said Dr. Normandy.

He dropped to one knee, removed the backpack from his shoulders, and unzipped it to reveal a folded blanket.

"A blanket or tarp can calm a colossal cat such as this down. The trick is to get the blanket over his head," said Dr. Normandy.

"He's down now, so that won't be difficult," replied Daryl.

Tegan walked up and kneeled beside Dave. She placed a hand on his massive shoulders and stroked his head.

"The trick now is we have to get him to the cage in the truck's bed. I'm not sure it will be large enough to hold him. This boy is a beast. The tallest and longest cat I have ever seen," replied Dr. Normandy.

"How long will that sedative keep him knocked out?" asked Jacob.

"Not long enough to get him down the hill, loaded up, and driven to the sanctuary. But he will be down for a couple of hours. He'll be awake before I arrive in Center Point," replied Dr. Normandy.

"He won't give you any trouble," said Tegan as she patted his head. "He just wants to be in a safe place."

Daryl and Jacob surrounded the animal as they watched Tegan stroke its head just as Dr. Normandy covered it with the blanket.

"Wasn't there a side-by-side with a trailer down by the barn?" asked Dr. Normandy.

"Yes, I will run down and get it," responded Jacob.

As Jacob jogged through the pasture toward the barn, the hogs started to grunt and move out of the way. At the foot of the hill, Daryl kneeled to pick up the front paw of the sleeping beast.

"What do you think it is?" asked Daryl.

"We'll do some medical tests on him when we get to the Center, but my guess is he's a liger," replied Thomas.

"What the hell is a liger? That sounds made up," replied Daryl.

"It's an intentional cross-bred species of big cat," replied the doctor. "They are the offspring of a male lion and a tigress, and the largest cats on earth, dwarfing the size of either parent," answered Dr. Normandy.

"How can you be certain?" asked Tegan.

"Its face resembles a tiger, but it doesn't have a mane like a male lion. Lionesses mate with several male lions throughout their lives, so the male lion's genes are adapted to maximize the growth of his offspring, since his offspring may be required to compete with those of other males produced by the same lioness. Female lion genes are adapted to cancel or dampen the effects of the growth-maximizing genes of male lions, so lions remain within a size range. However, tigers do not possess the growth-limiting adaptations. As a result, the influence of the adaptations provided by male lions is greater, which allows ligers to become larger than their parents," said Dr. Normandy.

"Why couldn't it be a male tiger and a female lion?" asked Daryl.

"That would be a tigon, and those have growth-limiting genes found in both male tigers and female lions. That makes them a little larger than their parents, but by possessing an abundance of these genes, they have a smaller size. This guy I would estimate to be almost eleven feet from nose to tail, and well over a thousand pounds."

"How do you know someone intentionally bred this animal?" asked Daryl.

"In the past, it could be possible for them to mate in the wild. Ligers cannot exist in the wild because lion and tiger territories no longer overlap. Therefore, it had to be an intentional creation," replied Dr. Normandy. He reached down and picked up a leg in the middle of the animal as he pointed out, "Plus, this guy has six legs."

Headlights bounced over the landscape as Jacob made his way to the group in the side-by-side. The fourteen-foot trailer pulled behind it with a large white metal cage that rested on top of the trailer.

"Party bus has arrived!" called out Jacob.

"Now comes the trick. How can four people lift a thousand-pound cat and put it on the back of a trailer?" said Daryl.

"I've got the blanket around him," replied Dr. Normandy. "If we can get the cage to the ground and open it, we should be able to slide the blanket with him on it into the cage. Once we get him in and locked inside, we can each grab one of the metal handles and lift it onto the bed of the trailer."

The blanket slid across the metal bottom of the cage and allowed Dr. Normandy to close the door once the animal was inside.

"Ready?" Dr. Normandy asked as each member took position behind the metal handle and lifted.

Tegan's increased strength allowed the four of them to get the cage off the ground with Dave inside. It was still a struggle, but they could place it on the edge of the trailer and scoot it into place. Jacob took position behind the wheel, Tegan up front, with Daryl and Dr. Normandy in the back.

"Let's roll," said Daryl as Jacob turned the vehicle around and drove back to the barn.

Jacob backed the side-by-side up to the bed of Dr. Normandy's truck. The proximity allowed it to be an easy transfer from the trailer to the truck's bed. Daryl and Jacob climbed inside the bed while Dr. Normandy and Tegan lifted the front handles enough to scoot the cage forward and allow Daryl and Jacob to grab it. The two in the trailer moved to the back of the cage and lifted and then walked forward until the cage was inside the director's truck.

Back at the farmhouse, Miss Ellie walked outside to see the animal that had terrorized the farm for several days. The size of the creature surprised her, but she was grateful Tegan, and her assembled team of trackers, could locate and capture the beast and put an end to her fears of what lurked in the darkness. "I better get out of here and get this animal to the sanctuary. I am sure he will wake up in a bad mood before we get there," said Tom.

"He won't give you any trouble," said Tegan. "And his name is Dave."

"Dave?" asked Dr. Normandy. "How do you get that?"

"He told me," replied Tegan.

"Okay, then let's get going, Dave," Dr. Normandy said as he tapped on the top of the cage.

Dr. Normandy entered the truck and waved to the remaining investigators as he drove out of sight.

Sleep well, Dave. Thank you for cooperating with me. Enjoy your new home, thought Tegan as she watched the taillights disappear as Tom turned onto the road and headed to Dave's new home in Center Point. She turned to Miss Ellie, Daryl, and Jacob.

"It's time for me to get going as well," said Tegan.

"It was a pleasure," replied Daryl.

"I couldn't have saved my hogs without you," said Jacob.

"Round here we hug," said Miss Ellie, as she moved in closer to embrace Tegan. "I'm not sure why this animal was here and has been seen for over a hundred years, but it helps us get over the past and move forward with new hope and confidence that we are beyond the dark days," said Miss Ellie.

"I'm glad I could help. This adventure did a lot for me as well," answered Tegan as she opened the door to her Dart and prepared to drive back to her apartment.

As she merged onto I-69, she felt a different energy. The road that felt like a tumultuous, angry river now flowed calm and peaceful, as if the universe was happy. She enjoyed the thirty-minute drive home, where she planned to escape to the comfort of her bed for the rest of the night.

14 Antidotes To Poisons

The sun glowed in the bright blue skies of Center Point, Indiana. Eleven o'clock and the occupant of the straw bed in the new exotic feline enclosure stirred. Dave the Liger tried to shake the groggy feeling from his head. He rolled over onto his back and reached to stretch his six legs upward. Standing up, he stretched, and let out a grunt as he reached the maximum radius of his stretch.

He stood in the shadows of the building and scanned his enclosure. He saw trees, bushes, a metal water tub, and a couple of balls to play with. The temperature was unseasonably warm.

The enclosure reminded Dave of his home on the hill behind Miss Ellie's. There were trees where he could scratch his back and his claws. He took three cautious steps into the sun. Its warmth felt good on his face, despite the temperature of the outside air.

He studied the enclosure, and his first impressions were comfort and peace. He explored the area as he sniffed the air and pawed the ground. In the sun, he stretched again and let out a loud roar to announce his arrival. He walked over to the metal tub and took a long drink. He knew the water would help to remove the toxins from last night's sedation from his body.

Following his roar, neighboring cats walked toward their enclosure to set eyes on their new neighbor. A young tiger named Drago walked to a spot in his enclosure where he could see the newest resident. He returned a roar, not as loud as Dave's, but a response that welcomed him to the Center.

Snow covered the ground of the enclosure, and Dave laid on his back with his legs in the air. He wiggled from side to side, to scratch his back, and also to display his contentedness to his new home. He rolled over into a seated position and sneezed from the snow entering his nostrils.

He closed his eyes and smiled, as a sensation of comfort washed over his body, and he felt comfort as he thought about his new life and the opportunity to be himself.

Two hours south, the sun glowed through a couple of turned slats in the bedroom blinds of an Evansville apartment. Eleven o'clock and the occupant of the queen-sized bed stirred. Tegan Stone tried to shake the groggy feeling from her head. She rolled over onto her back and reached to stretch her arms and legs upward. Standing up, she stretched, and let out a grunt as she reached the maximum radius of his stretch.

The wooden apartment floor was cold to the touch of her feet. She looked to the floor and discovered the location of her woolen slippers.

She rubbed her eyes with the knuckles of her hands, then ran her fingers through the longer portions of her red hair. She enjoyed the freedom the shaved sides gave her, as well as the shorter time to get ready in the mornings.

She walked to separate the blinds and looked outside at the sunny morning. Her watch showed the temperature outside was unseasonably warm. It attempted to melt the snow from the sidewalks and parking lot.

She made her way into the kitchen and poured cereal into an empty bowl before she covered it with almond milk. As the milk settled into the cereal, she reached to her right and buried her hand into another bowl and then worked a fistful of gummy worms into her mouth.

She picked up the cereal bowl and made her way toward the bedroom, stopping prior to exiting the kitchen, she backed up to the door jam. She wiggled from side to side, to scratch his back, and also to display his contentedness to her new life.

Continuing her journey back to the bed as she enjoyed the comfort of her homey apartment. She thought back over her adventure in Owensville and was happy to have not only helped Miss Ellie and Jacob prevent further loss to their hogs, but she also took comfort in being able to communicate with Dave the Liger and ensure his safety and relocation to a new home.

She climbed back into bed, pulled up the Untappd app on her phone, and searched for Strangeways Brewing Wampus Cat Triple IPA. As the search found its target, she looked at the image of the can, an enormous cat with a third eye. A sign that it was an intuitive, sentient higher being. And Dave was that. A being who could communicate with Tegan thanks to her newfound powers. Powers granted to her by the strange Pukwudgie, Puddlesquat and the Necromancer, Santiago Torres.

Without them, she wouldn't be here today. But she was, and she emerged from death with a new sense of strength, confidence, leadership, and unafraid of death. She was fierce, she could telepathically communicate with humans and animals, she could see the outcome of conflicts before they occurred, and could help guide people toward their true, often unrealized, selves. The future was full of hope, and Tegan was full of confidence.

She closed her eyes and smiled, as a sensation of comfort washed over her body, and she felt comfort as she thought about her new life and the opportunity to be herself.

She opened her eyes, looked down at her watch, and smiled again. She turned to the side and reached into the top drawer of her nightstand and removed a stack of papers. She read the top paper, flipped through the stack, and laid them back on her bed. The apartment's lease papers fanned out.

A feeling of happiness overwhelmed her. She picked up the phone, searched for a name from her contact list, and pressed the name to dial. It rang three times before a voice on the other end picked up.

"Hello."

"Hi, Jourdyn…" replied Tegan.

to be continued

Beer List

Against the Grain Brewery Bo & Luke Stout - Imperial / Double

Cerveceria Kross Golden Pale Ale - International

Damsel Brew Pub Lizzy Berliner Weisse

Miller Brewing Company Miller Lite Lager - American Light

New Day Craft Mead & Cider Three Eyed Magpie Mead - Fruited

Oliver Winery Camelot Mead - Fruited

St. Benedict's Brew Works Dark Souls Belgian Quadruple

St. Benedict's Brew Works Sign of the Dragon Farmhouse Ale – Saison

Strangeways Brewing Wampus Cat Triple IPA

Vincennes Brewing Company Fat Cat Triple IPA

Vincennes Brewing Company RendezBrew Pilsner - Other

About The Author

Mark Trollinger is a fan of cryptozoology and craft beer. He grew up in Yellow Springs, Ohio and attended the University of Rio Grande in Rio Grande, Ohio - not far from Point Pleasant, WV, thus igniting Mark's interest in cryptozoology, beginning with Mothman. In 2012, Mark first tried Stone Brewing's Russian Imperial Stout, thus igniting Mark's interest in craft beer.

He is the author of *The Chupacabra and the Bat Rastard*, *Champ and a Bit of Sunshine*, *The Red Ghost and a Chocolate Bunny*, *The Loveland Frog and the Narrow Path*, and *Tegan Stone and the Gibson County Beast* - all books in the Texans Investigating Mysterious Entities (T.I.M.E.) cryptozoology and craft beer adventure series.

Tegan Stone and the Gibson County Beast is a supplemental title in the T.I.M.E. Agency series

Myths and Malts Website

Mark Trollinger's

Amazon.com Author Page

Words From The Author

While working on The Loveland Frog and the Narrow Path, I knew the direction going into book number five. As I neared the end of the Loveland Frog, it changed. My original plan was for Tegan to be attacked by the visitors and swallowed, but Kareem saves the day with the actions he took. They would save her before any serious damage occurred. Then I added the wrinkle of her dying during the conflict.

Several months ago, I was working on ideas regarding other new books, not part of the T.I.M.E. series. I thought of a necromancer who finds people in the astral plane and returned them to Earth. When I finished Loveland, I decided I wouldn't write an entire story about that guy. At least not yet. Then idea crept in, why not include him in this one? If did write a story about him, he would need someone to retrieve, and Tegan was in a precarious position. So she died, only to be revived by the character who later became named Santiago Torres.

Another thing that happened in leading to this novella occurred around the same time. I read an article by Jon Webb on Courier & Press where he included four creatures around the Evansville area. I picked Evansville, as it was close to Cincinnati, which is where we last saw Tegan. Jon listed The Gibson County Beast as one of these creatures. I could not locate any other mention of the creature, but I liked it and wrote a story about it.

This book is a solo adventure and not fully a part of the T.I.M.E. series, at least in terms of numerical sequence, it is a supplement to the T.I.M.E. universe and fitting between books four and five.

Field Notes

Cover

The design of this cover was created by Nyssa Iniguez. She has redesigned the first four books in the T.I.M.E. Agency series.

Dedication

I have been fortunate to have many strong, independent women in my life. Women who do not back down from adversity and overcome whatever the odds to achieve their goal. My mother is one of the first models. She has always moved forward in life, taking on any challenge she faced. After a divorce from my father, and following my college undergraduate graduation, she enrolled in a college program. She started with an associate degree and did not stop until she was Dr. Trollinger, an academic textbook contributor, conference speaker, and university professor. My wife Susana has been a fighter her entire life and fought for her mother and children as a single mom, never stopping. She is strong and independent, yet grateful and always willing to help not only her friends, but random strangers. With the lessons of my wife and her mother, my daughter Karmina is becoming an example as well. Both of my grandmothers: Mary Lou and Ginny, my friends Sobie, Marsha, Ronda, Holly, Kristina, my ex-wife Maggie, and many other women in my life are also examples of a modern-day Valkyrie. I love to watch the WNBA, especially the Phoenix Mercury. Diana Taurasi is a modern-day Valkyrie.

Chapter 1

Some time has passed since the conclusion of *The Loveland Frog and a Narrow Path*. This chapter introduces confusion surrounding the events of book four. Many near death experience survivors describe changes in behavior, personal tastes, and habits • I liked the idea of thinking about the highway as a river. Sometimes it is fast and angry, and other times it is calm and peaceful. I think of this daily when I drive in to work.

Chapter 2

We learn Tegan has been seeing a therapist while staying in Evansville to help find resolution to her questions. Dr. Ollie uses a handshake technique introduced by Milton Erickson to ease her into hypnosis by shocking the subconscious through disrupting this common social norm • We learn about her childhood, including being raised by a single mom and having a brother and a sister. She had to help her mother with the kids, showing that she was always willing to sacrifice to help others • Tegan disclosed how she also battled feelings of being insufficient and weak, demonstrating Imposter Syndrome. Dr. Ollie reassures her and attempts to instill confidence.

Chapter 3

It is interesting how things randomly connect. Thinking of the character Santiago Torres and coming up with background information, I started by thinking he liked soccer. Where, I didn't know. Could be anywhere in the world. I picked the Santiago Wanderers soccer team in Chile Primera. Then I realized that's cool, because his name is Santiago. Maybe that's why he likes them. When I came to this chapter to introduce him, I tried to decide where he lived. If his power is astral projection, he didn't have to live in Indiana so where? Since he liked Chilean soccer, why not Chile? • Next, I searched for Chilean towns and thought Puyuhuapi sounded cool. Where would he work? I found limited information but turned to Google maps and zoomed in on the area. There were a few restaurants, so why not there? I zoomed into a part of town that had restaurants and found they were on a road named Carretera Austral. Then I realized that was perfect because Austral also returned search results for astral projection, which is what this character did. Chile also fit into including DMT. I didn't know until I read an article by Mayra Alejandra Bonilla that not only was DMT prevalent in Chile, but its demand was growing, and police confiscated synthetic versions of the drug. • **Don't do drugs, kids.** • Multiple random factors lead to a connection to the story. That happens more than I expect across this series. • At the time of this writing the exchange rate of $10,000 Chilean pesos was $12.31 US dollars • A rumor about the Enchanted Forest is that it is home to gremlins, and I felt Puddlesquat could somewhat fit that description • Maybe one day we learn more about these Rocemur from Canter's Cave (maybe Book 12).

Chapter 4

Chapter four gives us a look at Tegan's dreams. I wanted to introduce the idea that Santiago and Puddlesquat are connected to Tegan, and they visit her dreams. These are lucid dreams where Tegan is an observer of her encounter in Loveland, and we put pieces of the puzzle together to show what happened in the space in time after a Xeephin ate her and before she came to in the forest • As I edited the story I realized spell check had an issue with various forms of the word Xeephines. To differentiate various forms, Xeephines became the name of the collective group, Xeephine the general form of the race, and Xeephin became the name for a specific, singular individual • Including the soccer game on television and the team being the Santiago Wanderers was another way to connect her to Santiago Torres • I decided in each dream sequence for this and future chapters Tegan would eat a snack late at night because one characteristic she has from prior books is that she has the appetite of a competitive eater. That personality trait remains in her character after Loveland.

Chapter 5

A Change Is Gonna Come is the title of a Sam Cooke song, but also represents a theme of this chapter • I liked the idea that she was looking in her mirror, thinking about the dream, and realizing she had different feelings now, but not saying anything. Then the next paragraph she is in a stylist's chair making a change • Tegan once again has dreams that reveal more of the puzzle to what happened to her after Loveland. • The changes in her behavior and tastes, like many people feel after Near Death Experiences, show in her changes in hairstyle, clothing choices, taste in music, and getting a tattoo • The tattoo artist shows her two tattoo designs they have discussed in communication not included in the story. Both relate to Norse folklore and are symbolic of her new self • One change shown was the new perfume because that was the key to what happened to her in Loveland • I liked the end of the chapter because it shows her observing the ending battle in Loveland. She assumes that while she is lucid, everything else in her dream was just a replay of events. That's when Puddlesquat shows he also can have lucid activity. A startling way to wake up and end the dream sequence • In prior books I worked in obscure words. In this chapter we get nodus tollens and rückkehrunruhe • The Inkubus tattoo shop is a fictional store that I created, thinking Inkubus was like incubus, and a tie to mysteries entities •

The record store Vinyl Forest is also fictional. • I used the name Agnete for the tattoo artist because it is Norwegian, and it was an attempt to nod to the future revelations in the story.

Chapter 6

This chapter is lengthy. Tegan has her first beer in months. She acknowledges that in the past, when she felt stumped, the local brewery was a good place to clear her head and work through her problems, but after all the changes she's experienced, she isn't sure if she still likes beer. I worked in a quote from Judge Kavanaugh during his confirmation hearing because I felt it was funny and it fit here • We learn Tegan does still like beer, but her tastes have changed. She goes with her old standby, the Berliner Weiss, and while she does like it, she now prefers other styles • The bartender offers her mead, and she discovers it gives her visions. This is a tie in with the folklore of the Valkyrie who brewed and served mead. She doesn't learn that is what she is yet, but receives an incoming mental transmission gives us a voice in her head. That leads her to discover Santiago and Puddlesquat • We get an extended journey into a description of what happened in Loveland • We learn Puddlesquat knew how the battle would turn out and cast a protective spell over her She died at the hands (or mouth) of the Xeephin, and following death, entered the astral plane. In Chapter 3, we learned that happens to dead people. Because the energy from Puddlesquat protected and marked her, he could send Santiago to bring her back to earth. Although it seemed like just a few second on earth, it was a longer process because time is not linear, as we find out • We learn about Tegan's grandmother, her abilities as a Valkyrie, and how she saved the Pukwudgies in a battle with the Jersey Devil (more to come on that in the future) • In saving the Pukwudgies, Puddlesquat felt a debt to Tegan's grandmother. Because he has grandma's powers, he knew Tegan would die, and set out to save her to repay the debt • There is a lot of information coming in here, but Tegan is not afraid or overwhelmed. Now that she is a Valkyrie, she is no longer timid.

Chapter 7

Another cryptid in the area surrounding Evansville is the Spottsville Monster, a relative of the Sasquatch. I worked it in here as a nod to the creature, but also to show her ability to communicate with animals. The concept came from an article by Makia Freeman entitled Animal

Communicators Prove It's Possible to Hear an Animal's Thoughts. I felt it was an interesting concept and it would be useful in future cryptid adventures • Santiago told Tegan in Chapter 6 about three practices modern-day Valkyries follow, one being Shinrin Yoku, which is to be in nature and connect with it to refresh. The park is a place the Spottsville Monster has been reported and provided an excellent opportunity to practice that and meet the Monster, or Allutus, as he calls himself.

Chapter 8

The Iron Horse is a bar by the railroad tracks just a few miles outside of Owensville. It is a popular local hangout where Tegan could find potential witnesses to begin her investigation. Ronnie tells her about an experience he and his friend Jerry had while riding their motorcycles near Owensville one day. Matt is another biker at the bar who overhears the conversation and mentions his friend Daryl saw the creature. Giving both men her number, she plans to meet with each • Daryl calls her that evening but doesn't want to discuss over the phone and asks her to meet him and another friend at a different bar the next day • We also get some historical accounts about the unknown animal called the Gibson County Beast, as Ronnie describes the 1935 account of J. Oscar Hunt. This sighting was the appearance described in the Jon Webb article • Unbeknownst to Tegan and Daryl's friends we met at the Iron Horse, it wasn't the first time he encountered the animal.

Chapter 9

Each of the chapters to this point have focused on Tegan's discoveries and mentions of the creature in the paper or eyewitnesses. There hadn't been a scene that features the animal in action in the community. This one is short, but its purpose is to show that the animal is in the community and is a threat.

Chapter 10

The meeting place Barrel & Barley is a fictional bar • Tegan meets Daryl and his friend Cody to talk about their sighting • This friend is not a biker like Daryl's other friends. Instead of the big domestic beer that most of his friend's drink, Daryl enjoys the occasional craft beer with Cody while watching rodeo • The rodeo is a tie in to book five in the series • We learn more about what Daryl saw. We also discover these two guys who appear wouldn't have anything in common, both enjoy craft beer and watching rodeo. That suggests to us to get out in the world and meet people, even if you don't think you have common interests. We often have more in common with others than we realize • We get more details on the 1935 sighting of the Gibson County Beast as well as a mention of an earlier sighting in the early 1900s • The discussion about the creature leads to the disclosure of a 1908 sighting. Here I attempted to tie that sighting to the present day by having it connect to the same family. The 1908 sighting is from a similar sighting of an unknown animal also from Indiana, but not associated with the Gibson County Beast. Because there were so few sightings of the Gibson County Beast, I brought in a similar story of an unnamed creature • Daryl is a guy who is into shows about Bigfoot, and he's leery about the government hearing or following him. He warns Tegan that she might encounter government involvement if she keeps looking into these unknown creatures. As Tegan leaves, we see a person wearing StarShield clothing take notice of her • I created a timeline for the two families, the Orr's and the Saygers. The families named were witnesses to the 1908 Indiana sighting. Creating a family tree connected to that time put Miss Ellie's Grandma Clara in with the original lore, and allowed Tegan to see that Ellie's grandma, much like her own grandma, had secrets • To explain Clara being a widow, I worked in details about her grandfather going to Columbus, IN to buy hogs. They have hogs on their farm today, so I included his trip to Columbus as part of that story. But based on the timeline, I had to review the history of hog transportation during that time. There were no cars with trailers or semis then. There were a lot of trains or barges shipping hogs, which accidentally tied with Book 4. Cincinnati was one of the largest transporters at the time and why it was called Porkopolis • To explain why Clara's husband didn't return, I mentioned brief details of his demise. Police wrote it off as mischievous teenagers, but it happened in a city park where sightings of an unknown creature happened. The creature was called the Mill Race Monster. We may encounter it again in the future. • Miss Ellie states she knows what the creature is and calls it the Wampus Beast. Also known as Wampus Cat, it is a known Native American legend. The name Gibson County Beast gives way to Wampus Beast. This gives the ability to tie this animal to more encounters throughout the eastern and southern portions of the country.

Chapter 11

They set out to see where Jacob filmed the video of what he saw a few nights ago. Tegan comments on the size of the hogs. Jacob points out the largest pig on record as Big Bill, which is accurate. An interesting and unexpected tie here to the Loveland Frog is Jacob describing Big Bill as a Poland China. It is correct that those are an old and large, muscular breed of pig. I was unaware at the time those pigs were first raised in Lebanon, Ohio, which is close to Loveland. It provided a splendid opportunity to ask if Tegan had ever been to Cincinnati • The setting of Owensville and the number of farmers within the community who rely on livestock for their living provides a similar account for Tegan to connect to the setting in the Chupacabra (Book One).

Chapter 12

Liminal means, *Of or pertaining to an entrance or threshold* or, *Of or pertaining to a beginning or first stage of a process*. It seemed like a good name for the first investigation as a team with Tegan, Daryl, and Jacob • The three investigators made good progress, but evening approached, and they had to leave. Back in her apartment, Tegan searched for answers to the Wampus Beast and for local help in identifying the creature • The sent video by Jacob convinced the director to help with the investigation.

Chapter 13

This chapter is the final investigation of the Gibson County Beast, or Wampus Beast. Dr. Normandy showed up to assist with the investigation • To celebrate and bring good luck, Daryl purchased a bottle of what he thought was wine, but it was a local Indiana mead. The mead caused Tegan's visions to kick in, and she sensed the animal on the hill. Seeking to communicate with the animal, she made contact. Realizing this was a sentient being who was only trying to stay out of sight and survive, she knew they could not kill it • Dr. Normandy stated he had a thought, for some unknown reason, to pack the tranquilizer gun as he prepared to drive to Owensville • Tegan convinced Dave to work with them and sold him on the benefits of living in a Sanctuary. Dave agreed and allowed them to approach close enough to use the darts • The beast's name is unusual for an unknown creature. The name Dave was used because of a Twitter post I made while writing the scene. I struggled with a name and asked what a lion-like animal would say its name was if it could know its name. There were a few responses to the question, but the one that stood out was a responder who said, "I would like to think it's Dave." And so it was • The Exotic

Feline Rescue Center is an actual place, and I selected it based on the geography of the story. They do great things there with rescued big cats • If you have read Books 1-4 after autumn 2022, you have seen a mention of a percentage of sales go to a selected non-profit organization. Those editions had that added during the revision to the current size format. The idea of tying the story to donations to a non-profit began with the initial publishing of this story. I selected the Exotic Feline Rescue Center because of the use of it in the story, and I thought it was a great way to give back. Since this original release, I added that feature to all future stories, and I edited the prior books to include it • If you would like to sponsor a cat with the Exotic Feline Rescue Center in Center Point, Indiana, use your phone to scan the QR code below:

Your $50 donation goes toward the care of your selected cat. In return for your support, you will receive a 5" x 7" photo of your sponsored cat and two day passes to the EFRC. That program is not something I created, but is part of what they offer. I am just pointing it out • In deciding what Dave is, Dr. Normandy theorizes he is a liger, because of his size. He must be an intentional crossbred animal because lions and tigers no longer share the same habitat in the wild. He also points to the fact that Dave has six legs as a clue • I do not explain it who would create a six-legged liger, or why, but Dr. Normandy mentions a story of an escaped animal in Alabama. The locals claimed the government tried to create a Wampus Cat-like creature that escaped a facility and now roams the lands. According to The McDowell News in a 2009 article entitled Mike Conley's Tales of the Weird: Legend of the Wampus Cat, the government used a facility in remote Alabama to create a fast and fearless creature that would be used in World War II as a kind of messenger. This connects to Daryl's thoughts that the government may be behind the increase in cryptid sightings in chapter 10. Maybe we will find out more about that later.

Chapter 14

The story concludes as most of the T.I.M.E. books do, with a final refection. I began with Dave the Liger reflecting on life in his new home. He observes it, decides it is a safe and cool place, and he felt happy to be able to be himself. I repeated the same sequence and attempted to use nearly the same words when repeating the same thoughts from Tegan. She too has a new home, thinks it's a cool place, and she is happy, but still learning to be her new self. Unlike Dave, she reaches into a nightstand beside her desk and sees that it is nearing time to renew her lease on the apartment. She thinks about it for a moment, then picks up the phone to call someone. She says Jourdyn, and that's where the story then cuts out. That's a cliffhanger, that leads us into Book 5.

Beer List

The beer list in this story is much shorter because it is just one main character. There are a lot of great beers in Indiana, notably anything from Three Floyds, especially their Dark Lord variants. I didn't include those this time because I tried to keep this list to a small area around Evansville.

Newsletter

If you would like to sign up for the monthly newsletter where you can receive updates on new releases, public appearances, and the opportunities to preview and provide feedback as a beta reader, please enroll on my website with the QR Code below:

Other Interactive Opportunities

In addition to the **#chupacabraselfiechallenge,** there are other opportunities to interact with me as well as other readers of the series.

Most of the interactions occur on Instagram, but you could use other social media pages. Check out my page at **https://www.instagram.com/mark_trollinger**

Do you like those daily photo challenges that provide a list of themes at the beginning of the month, and you respond by posting a photo representing your interpretation of the photo prompt? If so, **#Chupacabradailyphotochallenge** is for you.

Maybe you enjoy locations named in the books? The series does occur in the real world, so you can visit the places named. Take a photo of the location, maybe even include yourself in the scene. Post it to Instagram with the hashtag **#ScenesfromtheTIMEAgency**

Do you like craft beer? If you're reading the series, I hope you do since it is one of the major themes. Each book contains a list, alphabetical by brewery, in the book matter pages. If you are drinking one of the books listed, why not post a photo of the beer next to the book and put it on Instagram with the hashtag **#BeersoftheTIMEAgency**

In my opinion, these are fun ways to enjoy the book one another level and get to know others who enjoy the series. I would really like to build up the community and meet you on the road at an upcoming event!

 # Photo Challenge

Another way I wanted to make this series interactive was to use one of those daily photo challenges consisting of a word or phrase related to the book. Readers could post a daily photo to their Instagram page with the hashtag

#chupacabradailyphotochallenge and we could see what other readers are posting. I will start this up in January 2023. Check out my Instagram page for details: mark_trollinger.

Sound Booth

During the writing of this story I listened to some hardcore music like **Code Orange** and **Incendiary**. I found I liked both and recommend them.

Other style I listened to a lot of during this story was Scandinavian, I guess they call it folk music, especially **Heilung** and **Wardruna**. Surprisingly, both are coming to Phoenix in the fall of 2022, and I have tickets to each show. Another artist that I listened to in the final days of this story and found that it also fit the genre of Tegan's new taste in music is **Peyton Parrish**. I am unsure of his full body of work, but he has several songs related to Vikings and they sound cool.

You can get into the mood behind the story by listening to the playlist I put together.

Tegan Stone Spotify Playlist